Praise for *Dead Dog*

"Max Davis's writing exudes charm and acce
combination of honesty, humility, optimism,

Publishers Weekly

"Powerful, powerful book! Lives will be changed!"

Gary Stewart, *New York Times* Best-Selling author of
The Most Dangerous Animal of All

"Max Davis is an amazing writer and one of my favorites. *Dead Dog Like Me* may be the best book he has ever written. The story is captivating and the message is life changing."

Richard Exley, best-selling author of over a dozen books

"*Dead Dog Like Me* speaks personally to the reader, resulting in a joyous hope! Max is gifted with the skills and ability to share a story in ways that connect immediately to a broad audience, quickly drawing the reader into the heart of the book."

Mark Lubbock, pastor, regional director,
Iron Sharpens Iron National Men's Conferences, CEO, Gulf South Men

"Max Davis is a gifted communicator. He has woven together a little-known but powerful passage from the life of King David with a heartwarming contemporary story of loss and redemption to create a fabulous parable of how God's grace can change the life of a dead dog like me."

Mark Gilroy, publisher, blogger, and author
of the Kristen Conner Mystery Series

dead dog like me

dead dog like me

a novel

MAX DAVIS

WORTHY®
PUBLISHING

Published by Worthy Publishing, a division of Worthy Media, Inc., One Franklin Park, 6100 Tower Circle, Suite 210, Franklin, TN 37067.

WORTHY is a registered trademark of Worthy Media, Inc.

HELPING PEOPLE EXPERIENCE THE HEART OF GOD
eBook available wherever digital books are sold.

Library of Congress Cataloging-in-Publication Data

Davis, Max, 1960-
Dead dog like me / Max Davis.
pages ; cm
ISBN 978-1-61795-524-2 (softcover)
1. Traffic accident victims--Fiction. 2. Life change events--Fiction. 3. Mephibosheth (Biblical figure--Fiction. 4. Jonathan (Biblical figure--Fiction. 5. Saul, King of Israel.--Fiction. 6. Bible. Old Testament--History of Biblical events--Fiction. I. Title.
PS3604.A9726D43 2015
813'.6--dc23
                          2015002769

Scripture quotations are taken from the Holy Bible, New International Version®, NIV®. Copyright © 1973, 1978, 1984, 2011 by Biblica, Inc.™ Used by permission of Zondervan. All rights reserved worldwide. www.zondervan.com

Published in association with Ted Squires Agency, Nashville, Tennessee, tedsquires.com.

For foreign and subsidiary rights, contact rights@worthypublishing.com

ISBN 978-1-61795-524-2 (softcover)

Cover Design: Smartt Guys design
Interior Design: Bart Dawson

Printed in the United States of America
15 16 17 18 19 RRD 5 4 3 2 1

What is your servant, that you should notice

a dead dog like me?

—

2 Samuel 9:8

1

The emotional pain had morphed into physical symptoms. I didn't really want to die. I just wanted the hurting to stop. Gasping for breath, I felt my heartbeat quicken and my chest squeeze as if trapped in a wrenching vise. Sweat oozed from my pores, trickling down my body and causing the sheets to stick. After tossing and turning, I finally kicked free of them and lay still, trying to cool down. The breeze from the ceiling fan blew over my damp torso, creating a chill. I jerked the sheet back over me and twisted but couldn't get comfortable so I just sat up in the bed.

Out of the corner of my eye I could see the green glow from the digital clock, but I didn't need to look. I knew the time. They always came between 2 a.m. and 3 a.m. when I'm the most vulnerable—the voices in my head ambushing me like a gang of merciless thugs with clubs and chains, beating me down.

"Philip would still be here if it weren't for you, Nick," one of the voices taunted. *"You know it's true. Abbi would still be here too. It's all your fault. Can't let anything ruin your precious little vision. But it's always been about you, hasn't it? Always about you. You're pathetic."*

"I hate you!" I yelled back at the voice, clutching my hair, yanking. After letting my torso drop back down on the bed, I stared up into the darkness and whispered, "God, where are you? Why aren't you helping me?"

"Seriously, Nick?" the voice mocked. *"You don't still actually believe God is listening, do you? If he is, he sure has a habit of not showing up when you need him the most. You prayed so hard. You were so sincere. When are you going to get it through your thick skull? God let you down, Nick . . . again. He couldn't care less about you, if he even exists at all. You're insane to believe he does. You've wasted your whole life believing this brainless nonsense. That's all it is, Nick, and you know it, brainless nonsense—pure drivel, a sham for the weak-minded. And you fell for it! Think, Nick, think. God's not there. If he was he would have intervened."*

Rocking back and forth in the fetal position, I shook as heaving sobs burst from deep within my core.

"Oh, quit your sniveling, Nick. You're disgusting. Just look at you. You should hate yourself. Lots of people hate you. If God existed he'd probably hate you too. He'd surely be disappointed in you. How could he not be? You've let him down so many times . . .

so many, many times. You're a fake, and you know it. God's punishing you. You deserve it."

With snot smeared across my face and a black cloud of depression suffocating me, I reached over to where Abbi normally lay, where I'd often turned for comfort through the years. My hand stroked the sheets as treasured memories flooded my mind. I longed to feel the warmth that told me she was there. We loved to cuddle. I'd lie on my side, scoot up against her, and gently caress her. With my face buried in the crook of her neck, I would breathe in her sweet aroma—a mixture of bath oil, lavender shampoo, and lotion. Her intoxicating scent always released my stress and calmness would follow. Abbi would chuckle and say, "I'm soothing your soul, Nick."

Now I reached for her pillow instead, pulling it to my face, inhaling the fragrant aroma. I'd instructed Maria not to wash the sheets or pillowcases for nearly two weeks now, knowing that when she did Abbi's scent would fade. It was already fading.

The pain of loneliness jabbed me again, a twisted knife to the gut.

"There is a way out, Nick," the voice purred, now velvety and seductive as if offering me a gift. *"Abbi keeps it loaded in the bedside table. You know where it is. You bought it for her. It's right there, in the drawer. It would be quick and painless. No more pressure. No more hurt. You'd be doing everyone a favor."*

Clinging to Abbi's pillow, I turned my head toward her bedside table. The glowing green 2:41 on the clock was the only light. *"Go ahead, Nick. They'll be better off without you."* The voice was relentless. I continued to stare, contemplating.

Time slowed to a crawl—still 2:41. *"You heard what Abbi said. She doesn't trust you. She doesn't respect you anymore. How could she? You're such a fake."*

I sat on the edge of Abbi's side of the bed. 2:42. My eyes were becoming acclimated and I let them drift around the room. Her favorite silk pajamas were still flung over a chair and a cluster of her necklaces hung from a hook on the dresser mirror, the green glow from the clock reflecting off of them. I was drawn particularly to the gold one with pearls running around it. Simple and classic, it had been a gift for our twentieth anniversary, from me. Abbi loved it.

"She doesn't love you now, Nick. It's over."

2:43.

Slowly, I slid open the drawer and fumbled around for the gun, a compact Smith & Wesson five-round revolver. Before getting my hands on it, I paused for a moment, considering.

"Come on, you coward! Get on with it! You know what you have to do. Put the gun in your mouth and pull the trigger! At least Philip had the guts to put an end to his misery."

Forcing sentiment out of my mind, I let out a numb sigh, closed my eyes, and pressed onward. Sight wasn't necessary for what was next. But just as my fingers brushed the leather case, hysterical barking in the hallway jarred me out of my trance. Deuce clawed frantically on the bedroom door. I popped up from the bed and yanked the pistol out of the case, knocking over a framed picture of Abbi, me, and the kids. The glass cracked into a web when it hit the floor.

"That's you, Nick. Always breaking things."

I jerked open the door, wielding the pistol in front of me. "Deuce!" I shouted, flipping on the hall light, irritated. "What is it, boy? Geez, you're so hyper!"

Our family dog pushed against my legs and circled around me, his barking intensifying as if he wanted me to follow him.

"Calm down. I'm right here!" Deuce rarely barked and usually slept through the night. Something had definitely stirred him. We had put up a six-foot-high, wrought-iron fence with electric gates and installed a top-of-the-line security system. When you're a high-profile figure like me, privacy and protection become issues. It would take an act of God for any unwelcome guests to break into the Gregory compound. Still, I wasn't taking any chances and figured I'd better check it out.

"What, boy? Show me."

Still barking, Deuce started down the hall, glancing back at me to make sure I was coming. Shirtless, in my boxers, with the pistol leading the way, I followed, turning on lights as we went. The dog made a beeline to the double French doors that opened directly to the backyard patio and pool. At the door, he continued to bark frantically at something outside. I turned on the patio and pool lights, eased my finger on the revolver's trigger, and slowly stepped through the doors with Deuce on my heels and now growling. "Shh," I said, listening for anything out of the ordinary. I searched the patio and swimming pool, then peered behind the stone waterfall fountain on the pool's far end. Nothing was out of the ordinary, so I continued scanning our serene, well-landscaped backyard. Again, nothing was moving except the bugs flying around the yard lamps. I stood still for a moment. The sounds of crickets blended with the hum of the air-conditioning unit. Deuce immediately calmed down, so I figured whoever or whatever it was had run off.

"I guess you saw a ghost, boy," I said in nervous jest, knowing full well he'd sensed something. The whole ordeal was bizarre. I'd never known him to act that way. I tried to reason it was probably a raccoon or armadillo that had come out from the woods backing up to our property. We'd had problems with them. The security system had a motion detector that overlooked animals up to a certain weight. *I'm sure that was it,* I mused.

I bent over and stroked the rust-and-white furball of energy with one hand, holding the pistol in the other. "It's okay now," I said to the dog, trying to reassure myself as well.

"You can still do it, Nick." The voice in my mind returned, poking me. *"It's not too late. Just put the pistol in your mouth."*

Suddenly, I held the revolver away from my body as if it were a rattlesnake coiled to strike. The fog was lifting from my brain and I was mortified at what had almost happened in the bedroom, what was still going through my head. Things had gone too far this time, much too far. Opening the gun's cylinder, I let the bullets fall into my hand. Then I pitched the gun and the bullets into the pool, watching them sink to the bottom like lead bricks.

Realizing Deuce's interruption had quite possibly saved my life, I bent back down and buried my face into the top of his cute little head. "Good boy," I said, giving him a firm squeeze. "Good boy. How 'bout a treat?" His ears perked up, and we both shuffled inside toward the kitchen. Out of the refrigerator, I pulled Deuce's favorite—fresh deli-sliced honey turkey. It was the special treat Abbi always gave him. I held up a piece but he only looked up at me with his sad black-button eyes, then lumbered off, curled up in his doggy pallet, and let out a sigh. I tossed the meat on the floor close to him.

"I miss her, too, buddy," I said. "I miss her too."

2

Giving up hope of any sleep, I headed to my study to try
to get some work done. One thing was for sure: I didn't want
to get back in that bed. Walking from the kitchen and down
the long hallway to my study, I did a quick mental inventory of
the upcoming day. I desperately needed to finish the revisions
to my latest manuscript. The deadline was less than a week
away. The publisher had forked out some major bucks for my
advance and was getting anxious about meeting the press date.
In addition, my appointment book was chock-full of people
with serious issues looking to me for answers.

"You have no business counseling anyone, Nick." The voice
in my head was back, poking, harassing. *"You're the one with
serious issues."*

"Yep, you're right," I said out loud, clenching my fists so tightly my fingernails dug into my palms. "I'm a basket case. I'm not just hearing voices, but now I'm talking back!"

"That's funny, Nick. You know what else is funny? If people knew what was really going on and your secrets, they wouldn't be coming to you for guidance. They certainly wouldn't be reading your books or going to your fancy church! You're just the blind leading the blind. It's all coming down, Nikky boy—'Mr. Spiritual, got-it-all-together man of God.' Everything you've ever worked for is all coming down."

"Give it a rest already!" I screamed, punching the hallway wall in frustration. Instead of hitting only Sheetrock, my fist connected seriously with a solid wall joist underneath. I heard something crack and it wasn't the wood. Pain seared through my hand as I hopped around, cradling my throbbing fist.

"That wasn't smart, Nick. But that's you, always reacting first, thinking after it's too late."

I swear I heard the sound of shrieking laughter. Now I was positive I was losing it. By the time I finally made it to the study my energy was depleted and my hand swelling.

Plopping into the chair, I rolled up to my desk and let out a deep sigh. My favorite Bible was lying there, its cover faded, pages worn. A gift for seminary graduation, it was like an old friend that had comforted and consoled me over the years. I ran my left hand over the leather and opened the book to read the inscription. The handwriting was meticulous and artistic, like calligraphy.

Congratulations, Nick! You've studied so hard and God is going to reward your faithfulness to his call. I'm honored to be your partner in life and ministry. We're a team and I can't wait to see all that God is going to do through us. Thank you for loving Jesus and me the way you do. Remember, "In all your ways submit to him, and he will make your paths straight" (Proverbs 3:6). That's a promise!

Love for life, Abbi

I closed the Bible and looked at it intently, pondering. My whole life had been built around that book. I'd preached thousands of sermons, officiated countless weddings and funerals, and counseled scores of people—all from that book. Leaning back, I surveyed the shelves lining the walls, filled with hundreds of theological and inspirational books I'd collected over the years. All the studying and obsessive reading, where had it gotten me? Did I believe a word of it anymore? I turned back to the Bible. I'd studied it for years, learning the Greek and Hebrew. I knew the promises. I'd stood on them, claimed them, and declared them from the pulpit. I knew in my mind *why* I believed. Yet I'd seen so much pain and suffering—had caused so much pain and suffering. Was it worth it? Despite all my success, after nearly three decades of ministry here I was in a broken pile, not wanting to live. Like the voice in my head suggested, had I wasted my life believing this nonsense?

I flipped on my Mac and gazed out the window. Outside, our long driveway wound through an umbrella of oaks down to the main gate that opened onto a quiet, tree-lined road in an upscale, garden-district neighborhood. Though we'd tried to keep our residential location as low-key as possible, I knew when some people drove by and slowed down, they were saying, "That's where Nick Gregory lives." At first it was exciting, but things change. It's fun when everybody loves you, when you can do no wrong, but make a few mistakes—or a string of them—and you wish they'd never heard your name.

Suddenly I had the eerie sensation that someone or something was watching me. I spun the chair around cautiously and found Deuce, standing in the doorway, head tilted with a confused look that I interpreted as saying, *Why are you in your office at 3 a.m.? Why did you break the wall? When is Abbi coming home?*

Seeing his innocent, spry expression softened me—no pretense, no ego, just, *Here I am. This is me. If you don't love me, I'll still love you. Can we play now?* If only humans were more like dogs. If only I had been more like Deuce, then maybe Philip would still be here.

"You need some company, buddy?" I said, patting my left thigh and motioning for him to come.

At that, he jumped up in my lap. Stroking him with my good hand, letting his presence calm me, I thought again of my counseling schedule. Many of the big names came to see me: CEOs, professional athletes, head coaches, senators, congressmen, movie stars, and other high-profile ministers. You know, the important people. But they all had big problems and big

secrets to go with their big names. With the pressure to be po-
litically correct and the media sniffing around 24/7 like bloodhounds, no one in the public eye could afford to have cracks
in their facades, especially in this town. That didn't mean the
cracks weren't there—it was just as a matter of survival they'd
become experts at covering them. And if the bigwigs couldn't
reveal their cracks, then I certainly couldn't reveal mine. The
problem was, I didn't know how much longer I could last.
Keeping up facades and hiding secrets is hard, stressful work.
There's a saying in the counseling world: "We're as sick as our
secrets." It's true.

On top of that, I was dog-tired of the pressure to perform,
to smile, to always say the right words and do the right things.
I was tired of being under the religious microscope. I wanted
to be rebellious, to cuss somebody out and flip off idiot drivers.
I wanted to tell a few of the people I counseled the truth: they
were spoiled, rich brats who just needed to suck it up and do
the right thing! I wanted to grow my hair into a ponytail, get
a monster tattoo, then hop on a Harley and ride as far as the
open road would take me. But that wasn't going to happen.
I was Nick Gregory, *New York Times* Best-Selling author and
pastor of Grace Life Church, the largest evangelical church in
Washington, D.C., and the fourth largest in the United States.

What I really wanted more than anything was to hold my
wife, Abbi, in my arms again. I wanted to turn back the clock
for our son, Philip, too, to tell him I loved him unconditionally,

that he didn't need to be or do anything to gain my love and acceptance. Maybe if we had simply hung out more he'd still be here. But I was too busy writing important books, building my ministry, and counseling the important people. I'd resign the church, give back all my book royalties, and live in a cardboard box if it would bring my son back.

Deuce wiggled out of my lap and trotted into the foyer, then back toward the kitchen. *Just like a little kid,* I thought. *Can't stay still for long.*

Instead of opening my manuscript file as I had intended, I reached into my desk drawer again with my good hand and fished out the letter Philip had left a little over a year earlier. I'd read it dozens, if not hundreds of times, nearly every day since then. It'd become a ritual for me, a way of torturing myself. A private suicide note written just to me, Philip had hidden it where he knew only I would find it. There was no other note. That way when they found his body, they could not conclude suicide. I'd shared this letter with no one, not even with Abbi. That's one reason, the *main* reason she left. When she found what was written there, some of the reasons Philip did what he did, she was beyond furious. She felt betrayed . . . angry . . . devastated. Something snapped inside her. I knew it would. That's why I'd hidden the letter, apparently not well enough, though. Maybe subconsciously I wanted her to find it. Maybe I knew this was what I deserved. I remembered our conversation that night:

"*I did it for your protection,*" *I had told her,* "*and for the church's . . . it would tarnish our reputation, God's reputation. You know what people would think.*"

Abbi didn't buy it for a second. "*To protect me?*" *she'd screamed.* "*You did it to protect yourself, Nick! Your precious reputation!*"

I had moved closer to embrace her, to try to console her. That was a mistake.

"*Don't touch me!*" *she'd said, recoiling away.* "*You're a liar! You've been lying to me this whole time! I trusted you!*"

"*I didn't lie to you,*" *I had said.*

"*Oh, okay then, you only kept the truth from me! You all did! How many knew, Nick? The whole staff?*" *She'd jerked off her silk pajamas, flung them over the chair, and began pulling on her jeans.* "*Philip loved you so much! He was your son, Nick! Your son! And you betrayed him too! You betrayed all of us!*"

"*Abbi . . . I . . . I—*"

"*Just shut up!*" *she'd said through broken sobs.* "*Nick, what happened? You used to be our guy. Remember? We all depended on you. You were the one who fixed things and came through for us. There was a time when your family took priority over everything. Church, counseling, books—it didn't matter what it was, everything got put on hold if the kids or I needed you.*"

Her words had stung. I'm still that guy, *I'd thought.* "*Abbi, it's only been a year. None of us are thinking straight. We're still grieving.*"

"*You mean* I'm *still grieving,*" *she'd retorted.* "*Apparently you've moved on!*"

"That was low, Abbi." I had stood there, stunned, as she threw some of her things in a suitcase and walked out.

That was two weeks ago.

With quivering lips, I fumbled open my son's letter and began to read. Self-hatred and shame consumed me as I agonized over every word. My eyes fell on one particular line in the middle of the page, a line that had haunted me:

I'm sorry I disappointed you and God so much, Dad. I really—

Squeaking from down the hall grabbed my attention.

Deuce was heading back my way with a red squeaky ball in his mouth. He trotted into the study, dropped the ball at my feet, and looked up at me expectantly. How could he communicate so effectively without saying a word? If only I possessed such a gift.

"You do know what time it is, right?" I asked. The time on my computer screen read 3:37.

He just tilted his head like he always did, wagging his tail at lightning speed. I looked down at my right hand, which was still throbbing and sore, so I picked up the ball with my left, aimed as best I could, and tossed it awkwardly at an angle so it went through the doorway and down the hall. Deuce split after it like a greyhound out of the gates and then pranced back to me proudly. For me, the exercise was a brief reprieve from the heartache, almost as if Deuce knew I needed the distraction.

After the next toss, still avoiding doing any work, I slid the letter back in the desk drawer and clicked on my iPhoto program, bringing up a slideshow—snapshots of my family life all bunched together in a compressed computer file. I'd seen them hundreds of times, yet they never got old. Twenty-five years of images on a single megabyte. Abbi had scanned albums of pictures that had been taken before the digital age. They weren't in any particular order, and I let 'em roll. With each image that scrolled across the screen, a menagerie of emotions wrestled for supremacy in my mind. Why was I doing this to myself? I could easily click off the program. But . . . I couldn't stop looking. If could have grabbed a single one of those moments and gone back in time, I would have.

I paused on a picture of Abbi, me, and the kids. Carlee was eleven and Philip eight. We were in Hawaii on the beach. A happy memory. It was right after my first book was published and I had been invited to speak at a conference in Honolulu. The organization put the whole family up for six days. I'd speak once a day and the rest of the time was ours. Abbi looked amazing in her multicolored Hawaiian sarong. After thirteen years of marriage and two kids, she was still the most beautiful woman I'd ever laid eyes on. Her wavy auburn hair, fair skin, and radiant emerald green eyes could melt me. I touched the screen, brushing my finger across her face, remembering that day as if it occurred last week.

Clicking the mouse, the slideshow continued—pictures of the kids, T-ball, school plays, Christmases, birthdays, graduations—each image tugging on my heartstrings. Then a picture popped up of me appearing on the *Oprah Winfrey Show*. Even though I'm evangelical, Oprah was responsible for my breakout success as an author. After she endorsed my first book, it shot to number one on the *New York Times* Best-Seller list and remained there for over a year. My next three books followed suit—over ten million copies sold. It was crazy! Virtually overnight, Nick Gregory became a household name, a Christian celebrity. Offers and opportunities flooded in. The church exploded in growth. Our lives would never be the same. It was an exciting time, yet as I viewed the images of me with Oprah, what had seemed so important then was now hollow and empty. Yes, the money was nice—or was it? All that wealth and fame, what most people only dream about, couldn't keep our family together and our son here.

Next, one of my favorite pictures of Philip rolled across the screen. I pressed Pause again and carefully tossed the red ball out the door. Deuce took off. In the past it was just another picture of Philip, but over the last year it had become one of my favorites . . . and most agonizing. It was taken at his thirteenth birthday party. He was finally a teenager, and we'd made it a big deal. He wanted a paintball party so we reserved a paintball field and invited his friends. They had so much fun. Even the dads got into the action—all the dads except me, that is. Philip begged me to come, but I couldn't be there because I was off doing God's work somewhere. In the picture his buddies are huddled together with their arms slouched over each other, holding paintball guns, colored splotches of paint plastered all over their clothes. Philip was in the middle, helmet cocked up on his head, all smiles. It was the last picture of *that* Philip. Just a few months later he started smiling less and less, the innocent spark in his eyes turning distant and gray. As time passed, Philip spiraled downward, becoming withdrawn, angry, and defiant toward us, God, the church, everybody. We chalked it up to puberty and attitude. There I was, this great pastor and counselor, and I couldn't even pick up on my own son's desperate signals. We were the perfect Christian family. We had to be. Behind the scenes there were the scolding matches and threats, but come Sunday we were experts at putting on our masks, Philip included. He knew his role.

I was such an idiot.

"Yes, you were, Nick. And you put so much pressure on him. His whole life was about pleasing his amazing daddy. But you just had to push, didn't you? Remember right after he graduated, when you insisted that he preach in front of the whole church? You had those great plans for him. He wasn't ready. Yet you wanted him to get exposure—twenty thousand people plus the television audience. Well, he got exposed all right! And for what? So he could be just like you! That was too much on him. You should have known better. For crying out loud, Nick, he was only a kid! But he couldn't be a kid. He was carrying a deep, dark secret, and he was Nick Gregory's son!"

"Shut up!" I shouted at the voice. Anger boiled up from my gut, erupting, self-hatred and grief consuming me. Deuce returned, dropping the red ball at my feet. Instead of throwing it, I grabbed my treasured Bible and in a fit of rage hurled it across the room. The leather book smashed into a two-foot-high, hand-carved crystal statue of an eagle with its wings spread. Underneath on a bronze label were the words, *"They will soar on wings like eagles—Isaiah 40:31."* A gift for Pastor's Appreciation Day, the statue hit the wood floor with a loud *pop* and shattered. Deuce ran out the room and hid under a sofa. Observing the pieces of crystal scattered all over the floor, I felt more like a hideous buzzard than an eagle. "Forgive me, Lord," I whispered, knuckles still aching.

"That's really good, Nick. Better than the wall. You're gonna wreck the whole house at this rate! But it's par for the course, you breaking stuff. You need to clean up the messes you made."

I gritted my teeth, hardly believing what I'd just done, that I was even capable of such outbursts. I took a deep breath and slowly exhaled. As the last bit of air released out of my lungs, I heard two sharp yelps echoing off the foyer walls, followed by the sound of paws pattering on the wood floor toward my office. Deuce stopped in the doorway and let out another stern yelp. I had no problem interpreting his message.

I got up and he danced around my feet through the foyer with its thirty-foot ceilings and a mammoth chandelier to the massive front door. "I don't blame you one bit for wanting to get away from me, buddy," I told him. "I'd like to get away from me too. Abbi said she misses you. She's coming to get you soon and you'll be staying with her for a while." He wagged his tail enthusiastically and bolted out the door as soon as it opened.

"Looks like it's going to rain," I mumbled, heading back to my study. After tiptoeing around the broken crystal, I sat down in my chair and dropped my head on the desk.

3

The shrill chirping cut through the early morning silence.

My mind in a groggy haze, I scrunched open my eyes and reached for the phone on my desk. *Who's calling me at this hour? Nobody calls my landline anymore.* Then I remembered that I'd left my cell in the bedroom. I brought the phone to my mouth and garbled out the word, "Hello?"

"Nick, where are you?" It was Al Champion, my associate pastor and number-one cheerleader. His name fit him perfectly. Ex-linebacker for the Redskins, he was tremendously popular with a winning smile, yet at the same time he had an intimidating presence that could make the most defiant of men shake in their boots, especially with a four-inch-thick Bible in his hands.

"You should know," I shot back. "You're the one calling my house at this hour! Is something wrong?"

"Nick, it's eight forty-five! I've been calling your cell for thirty minutes!"

"What?"

"Yes! You missed the staff prayer meeting this morning and you're supposed to meet Lydia Rothschild here at nine! Please tell me you didn't forget. You know, she wants to talk *only* to you."

"Crap! I must have fallen asleep in my chair," I said, slamming my fist down on the desk, sending shock waves of pain through my right hand. Soreness had set in during my five-hour nap. "Son of a—!" I yelled into the phone, wanting to let out a string of expletives but bit my tongue.

"Pastor Nick! Remember, you're a church leader representing Christ."

Clutching my aching hand, I rolled my eyes and wished my fist could travel through the airwaves and smack Al right in the mouth. "Maybe she'll be late," I said.

"She's here . . . *with* her attorney."

"That figures," I said, leaping up from my chair. "Tell them I'm on my way and keep 'em entertained until I get there! Twenty minutes, tops."

"All right, Pastor," he groaned. "I'll try my best."

"Just do it, Al!"

I hung up and bounded out of my office, toward the bedroom. On about my third step, the ball of my bare foot came down with full force on a piece of jagged crystal, causing me to let out an unholy shriek. I jerked my foot up to yank out the shard of glass. Blood was spurting onto the floor so I pulled off my boxers, wrapped them around my wounded foot, and hopped buck-naked through the house in search of gauze and Band-Aids—the big ones.

"This is getting entertaining, Nick! First your hand and now your foot. Ha, ha. Don't slip!"

"Focus," I told myself, ignoring the voice in my head. "Just keep moving."

Lydia Rothschild was a billionaire widow who was strongly considering pledging a sizable portion of her estate to the church, an estimated twenty million dollars. Her husband had owned a chain of five-star hotels and was part owner of the Washington Nationals baseball franchise. A real estate tycoon in her own right, Mrs. Rothschild had gobbled up half of Fairfax County when it was still tobacco and cotton fields. At eighty-one, she still traveled and invested in stocks and real estate. More importantly, she'd had an experience with God and wanted her money to have an eternal impact. Lydia believed in our causes, particularly missions, and we certainly could use the funds. We could always use the funds. It took massive amounts to keep our mammoth ministry machine running. Along with inner-city outreaches, a drug rehab facility, and three crisis pregnancy centers, Grace Life sponsored relief programs and orphanages with schools in Haiti, India, and Africa, and was building more. We were a church reaching the world. Lydia's children, however, were fighting us tooth and nail for the money. They wanted to block the donation by having her declared mentally unstable, but I wasn't worried. We had a team of pit-bull attorneys retained for just those sorts of things. Really, the only one who could mess this up was me, and I seemed to be on a roll lately.

After quickly rummaging through the medicine cabinet, I realized we were out of gauze and big Band-Aids, or at least I couldn't find them. Go figure. If they were somewhere in this house our housekeeper, Maria, could find them, but she wasn't here. When Abbi left I gave her some time off. So I sprayed the cut with antiseptic then hobbled to the kitchen, opting to cover the bleeding wound with paper towels and duct tape. I folded a piece of Bounty over the gash and wrapped the tape around my foot. It worked! They say that duct tape can fix anything. I briefly wondered if it could hold together a broken marriage.

Instead of showering, I splashed water on my face and gargled. I pulled on some slacks and a golf shirt, then carefully slipped my loafers on my tender foot. After taking a couple of tentative steps testing the soreness, I was able to limp briskly to the Escalade. As soon as the painstakingly slow garage door gave enough clearance, I put it in Reverse and punched the accelerator, whipping into the driveway turnaround. Just as I slammed the gear into Drive and took off, there was a *ding* on my cell indicating a text message.

I picked it up and read. It was Abbi. *"Nick, we need to talk*

NOW. It's important. My flight gets in today. I'm coming to get some of my things. I need to know when you are NOT going to be there. I won't be alone. And remember, I'm taking Deuce with me. There's something else we need to discuss." No smiley face. No "Love you" or "Miss you." All business.

Nervously, I began texting a reply. *"What? Now you're afraid of me?"* The vehicle swerved as I typed and I jerked the wheel, continuing my text. *"I'm not the monster you're—"* Precisely at that moment the Escalade veered off the concrete and into a camellia bush situated between two oaks, flattening it. Bringing the vehicle to a stop, I threw my hands in the air and looked up toward the darkening sky. "What else is going to go wrong today?" I wondered out loud.

"That was close, Nick. Could have been a tree. You know better than to text and drive. You're gonna kill someone. Too bad it's not you! At this rate you're going to succeed. You know Abbi wants a divorce, don't you?"

The voice in my head had picked at one too many of my emotional scabs. By nature, I wasn't an angry person. This morning had been an anomaly. All my simmering frustrations had reached the boiling point. The best way I can explain what happened next is that I snapped. Instead of shifting into Reverse to get back onto the driveway, which would have been the sane thing to do, I kept it in Drive, slammed on the gas, and exploded forward over the bush out into the front yard. The yard was big, the size of a football field. Letting out frustration, I revved the engine to its max, spun the tires, and cut the wheel sharply, making several doughnut circles and flinging grass and soil everywhere. I was laughing . . . and crying. For a few brief seconds I was free! So what if the neighbors were watching! So what if people driving by were rubbernecking! Who cared! I was momentarily insane and it felt great!

Since the camellia bush was already flattened, I visualized it was me lying there and plowed back over it. When I did, I felt a strange bump as the front tire on the passenger side lifted and dropped. Seconds later, there was horrific yelping. A sickening sensation filled the pit of my stomach. Slapped back into reality, I slammed on the brakes and jumped out. "Deuce!"

He thrashed around in convulsions, dragging his back legs, and collapsed under an oak tree. Blood trickled from his mouth, and one of his back legs twitched. Everything seemed to move in slow motion as I tried to comprehend the scenario unfolding before me. Did I just run over Deuce? No. I couldn't have. This was not happening. It couldn't be . . . not after everything else. A stiff breeze rose up, raking along the tree branches, hitting my face. With it came a wave of nausea, bile burning the back of my throat. Thunder clapped and rain began drizzling steadily, soaking both of us.

Dropping to my knees, I tried to comfort my companion as best I could. "It'll be okay, boy," I said, stroking the top of his head gently. "It will. I promise. I can fix this."

Shivering, with dilated pupils and a weak pulse, he appeared to be going into shock. Deuce was hemorrhaging and his breathing was shallow. Still, I had to do something. He'd saved my life. I had to at least try to save his.

Deuce gazed at me with an expression of devotion—loving and loyal as always, but surely confused. *Why has my master done this to me? I know he loves me. He knows best. I trust him.*

4

Abbi regularly took Deuce for his checkups, shots, and teeth cleanings. As far as she was concerned, we were going to be responsible pet owners and our dog was going to be a healthy, happy dog. With the animal clinic only fifteen minutes away, the vet had practically become another member of the family. She also attended Grace Life. Everyone at the clinic was crazy about Deuce and pampered him like royalty.

The adrenaline pumping through my veins allowed me to push past my own physical pain and scoop Deuce into my arms. The blood from his wounds smeared my white golf shirt as I laid him in the passenger seat. His panting had slowed considerably and I reasoned he wouldn't last much longer, perhaps not even to the clinic.

"Hold on, boy," I pled, my voice cracking. "I'm gonna get you some help, okay?"

Spinning the tires, this time I bolted down the driveway, out the front gate, and through the neighborhood onto the main highway. Weaving in and out of traffic with the flashers on, I thumbed through my contacts for the animal clinic and pressed Call. After two rings someone picked up.

"Great Falls Animal Clinic," a female voice answered.

"Dr. Conroy, please. It's an emergency! This is Nick Gregory."

"Oh, Mr. Gregory. Yes. Dr. Conroy is right here."

I could hear the receptionist whisper, "It's Nick Gregory." Dr. Conroy took the phone. "Hello, Pastor Gregory, this is Dr. Conroy. How can I help you?"

"Deuce has been run over! It's bad. I don't know if he's going'to make it! I'm on my way to the clinic right now!

"Oh, no!" she exclaimed. "Where are you now?"

"I'm on Highway 7 almost to Georgetown Pike. Ten minutes!"

"I'll get things prepared," she said with urgency. "Drive up to the front doors!"

I told Dr. Conroy ten minutes, but I hadn't planned on rush-hour traffic. Now it appeared the trip was going to be more like twenty or thirty.

"Just a little bit longer, buddy," I said, gripping the wheel with my good hand and caressing him ever so gently with my tender one. "I'm going as fast as I can. We're almost there."

Deuce let out a weak whimper—a strained effort to respond—then went quiet. His eyes were fixed and glassy, saliva dripped from the corner of his mouth, fur wet and blood-soaked. If not for the slight rise and fall of his chest, I would have thought he was gone. I realize it's impossible to get inside a dog's head and know what he's thinking, but it seemed to me Deuce was holding on . . . for me? . . . for Abbi?

"I'm so sorry, little buddy, so sorry. I didn't mean to hurt you." My tears flowed freely. "I love you so much." And I really did love him, though my words seemed hollow and fake, the same way I felt inside. I said I loved people and preached God's love, yet I had no problem running someone over if they got in my way.

Stopped at a red light, sitting there waiting, the weight of it all hit me. My body began to break out in cold shivers and my head felt like it was going to burst into a million little pieces. Foot throbbing and knuckles purple, everything within me was screaming to shut down, give up. Instead, I kicked up the heater and pressed the accelerator when the light turned green. Determination to save Deuce was propelling me onward.

I knew Lydia Rothschild was waiting, that potentially millions of dollars for the ministry was waiting. But why the delay? For a dog? Was Deuce worth it? Reason said no. *Think of all the people who could be helped with that money, the souls saved, the mouths fed.* Yet I knew there was nothing more important to me at this moment than getting help for Deuce. Al could handle Lydia Rothschild. He knew what to do.

Glancing again at our beloved family pet lying there, I couldn't stop the memories from running through my mind. Eleven years of laughter, love, and companionship Deuce had brought to our family. In the beginning, I didn't even want a dog. "Who's going to take care of him?" I argued. "A dog requires a lot of attention and will distract me from my ministry." I couldn't afford to let that happen. "I don't have time for a dog," I declared adamantly to the family over and over. I could tell it made them sad, but I knew best. We were on an important mission in building Grace Life Church. We had a vision. I was focused on success.

Then one day Abbi and I were driving by a pet store advertising dog adoptions that day.

"Can we stop and look?" she asked hopefully, clapping her hands excitedly. "Pleeease," she begged, poking out her lower lip. "I only want to look."

"All right," I said in a moment of weakness. "I guess so. But remember, we're just looking."

"Yes." Abbi nodded. "We're just looking."

I knew better.

An hour later, against all my previous arguments, we'd emerged from the store proud owners of a puppy that was a mix of mutt and Jack Russell terrier. The smile that dog put on Abbi's face totally jazzed me. I was the hero. How could I protest?

When Philip and Carlee saw him you would've thought we'd brought home lifetime passes to Disney World! It was love at first sight. Abbi and I decided to let them come up with a name. Brother and sister teamed up for once and unanimously came up with Deuce. It was perfect.

From the moment we stepped in the house with that dog, our family was never the same. I was never the same. Oh, how wrong I had been. Instead of distracting me, Deuce brought joy and actually helped me focus. He became my companion and buddy. We connected. I could even say that he inspired my writing. I can't tell you how many times we'd be on one of his "sniff walks"—we called them that because Deuce enjoyed smelling new things so much—and at some point during the outing a profound idea would drop into my mind, an idea that would not have come to me sitting behind a desk. Several of those ideas became cornerstones to my bestsellers. Was that dog worth twenty million dollars? You bet! More than anything, though, Deuce was fiercely loyal and loved our family unconditionally. No doubt, he would fight to the death to protect us. Deuce took his role seriously, keeping the squirrels in our yard at bay. His love for us turned me into a dog lover.

The drizzle had turned into a downpour, so I flipped the wipers on high. With each swipe of the blade came waves of accusations, guilt, and shame, as I replayed the scene in the front yard over and over. *It's my fault again. I break things. I destroy things. I hurt the ones I love. I'm poison.*

The voice in my head taunted, *"I can't believe you ran down the dog, Nick! What did he ever do to you except love you? He's going to die now. You kill things. That's you, all right. Abbi's love for you is dead. And Carlee hates you now too. Wait till they find out you ran over Deuce!*"

My cell phone started ringing. It was Al Champion. I should have answered to tell him I wasn't coming in. Instead, I just let it ring. Thirty seconds later he left a voice message. I didn't listen to it.

5

With her blonde hair pulled into a tight bun, no makeup, and wearing green scrubs, Dr. Mary Conroy was waiting at the front door of the clinic when I drove up. A great veterinarian, she had found her true calling in life.

"Oh Deuce," she said, opening the passenger door, "what did they do to you?" Her comment cut to the quick of my heart as much as the jagged piece of crystal had cut my foot. After gathering him into her arms, she rushed Deuce to a waiting gurney and whisked him to one of the exam rooms while I followed. With great care, Dr. Conroy laid him on the table and inserted a prepared IV into his leg.

"This will help you rest, sweetie," she said calmly, trying to reassure him. Turning to me she explained, "The meds will counter the shock and lessen his pain. It'll put him to sleep and make it easier for me to assess his wounds."

It only took about a minute for the medicine to take effect. Deuce's eyes closed and his body went limp. Wasting little time, Dr. Conroy dove into her exam.

"Definitely has a broken hip," she said, feeling, poking. "Broken ribs. Pelvis is shattered. Several deep gashes that need stitches. He's going to need surgery."

"So he's going to live?" I asked.

"It's hard to say. I need to take X-rays and do a more thorough examination. He probably has some internal injuries. It's going to be touch-and-go for the next twenty-four hours."

Deuce was dying before my very eyes and I felt my last ounce of hope draining out of me. "What can I do?" I asked.

"Not much now but wait," she said while scribbling something on her chart. "And pray." She looked at me like I had some special line to God, like maybe because I was a big-time pastor my prayers wielded more power. At one time my prayers were powerful and effective. I would spend hours basking in God's presence. I loved to pray. But since Philip's death, I'd pushed God away. The voice in my head had accused God of abandoning me, but in my heart, I had abandoned God. "He needs to stay here for a while—two or three days minimum," the doctor continued. "I'll call you when I'm done and give you an update. When Deuce wakes up, he's going to want to see you or Mrs. Gregory. Many times when a pet in this condition sees a loved one it sparks them to life. When no one is there, they often give up."

I nodded numbly, realizing Abbi was going to be devastated yet again, that this was just one more reason for her to despise me. My thoughts were broken when the receptionist stuck her head into the room.

"Mr. Gregory," she said nervously, "I'm sorry to interrupt, but you need to come take a look at this. It's urgent."

"Urgent?" I asked.

"Yes sir," she replied.

Dr. Conroy glanced up from her exam. "You go ahead. I've got it from here," she said.

"Thank you, doctor," I replied. I walked to the table and kissed Deuce on his head. "Hang in there, buddy," I whispered then followed the receptionist into the hall. "What's this about?" I asked.

"This way," she said, leading me in the opposite direction of the lobby into another office. Walking to the window, she peeked through the blinds and then motioned for me to look too.

I peered into the parking lot, where a cluster of news vans and crews had gathered. They were scurrying about, setting up their equipment.

"Why is the news out there? Is this an 'adopt a pet' promotion or something? You guys shooting a commercial?"

"No sir," she said while looking down, preoccupied with her cell phone. "I think they are here to see you, Mr. Gregory."

"Me? Why?" My thoughts immediately went tó Lydia Rothschild. "Why here?"

"Uh . . . I think I may have a clue," the young receptionist said, holding out her cell phone for me to see with a troubled look on her face.

"What are you talking about?"

"See for yourself."

I couldn't believe my eyes. There it was, the whole episode, my moment of temporary insanity in the front yard captured on someone's cell phone—the Escalade smacking into the camellia bush, cutting circles in the grass, whirling around like an out-of-control teenager, running back over the bush, and most regrettably . . . my front tire rolling over Deuce, him crushed and writhing in agony. All of it uploaded on YouTube with the caption: "Megachurch pastor and author Nick Gregory runs down pet dog in fit of rage!" The video made me look like a madman, and worse, it had gone viral in less than an hour! Now it was going to be broadcast on all the major networks and become ammunition for every talk show from *Nancy Grace* to TMZ.

At that moment Dr. Conroy stepped into the office. "What's this about?" she asked sharply. "What are all those news crews doing in my parking lot?"

The receptionist handed her the cell phone and Mary watched in horror while I stood by her side shell-shocked. When the sixty-seven-second video of my rampage had finished, she glared at me with fire in her eyes.

"It was an accident," I protested. "I didn't know Deuce was under the bush. I swear!"

"Does Mrs. Gregory know about this?"

I stood motionless a second, looked at the floor, then up at her. "If she doesn't yet, she will," I finally said. My chest tightened and the nausea returned, along with the burning bile rising in the back of my throat. I limped toward the front doors to meet the bloodhounds.

6

As if I were diving off a rocky cliff into the ocean, I took a deep breath and burst through the glass doors of the clinic. Holding my head down like an injured fullback who refused to leave the game, I limped through the throng of reporters toward the Escalade. It was only a short distance from the doors of the clinic to the door of my vehicle but not short enough. The reporters crowded into every available inch. With microphones shoved in my face and cameras flashing, multiple questions were hurled at me. I squinted my eyes just as a mic slammed me in the lip.

"Why did you run down your dog?" the female reporter demanded.

"Is the dog dead?" another one shouted.

"Is it true that your wife left you?" one yelled from a distance.

"Are you going to resign from the church?" came from the middle of the group.

Like rocket-propelled grenades, the onslaught of questions continued. Ruthless, the reporters didn't care about my pain. All they wanted was a scoop, a story, a sound bite, something sensational to get ratings.

"Some are suggesting your son was a victim of abuse."

"Was it suicide?"

"People are calling you a hypocrite. Don't you want to respond?"

"Did you have an affair? Is that why your wife left you?"

That one got me, piercing me to the core. I stopped and whirled around, right in the female reporter's face. "Get this straight," I shouted, waving my purple, swollen hand in her face while grabbing the door handle with my left, "I love my wife and have never once been unfaithful!"

"Why did she leave then?"

"She's vacationing," I said. Technically it was true. I wasn't lying. Abbi was taking some time at our vacation home in Fort Myers so she could think through some things.

The reporter rolled her eyes. "Does she know about the dog?" she poked. Glancing down, I caught a glimpse of Deuce's blood along with a patch of his rust-and-white fur on the bumper. My heart sank.

"Don't you people have any shame?" I said, opening the car door and climbing inside. I locked the doors, sealing me behind the tinted windows. I wanted desperately to slam my foot on the gas pedal and squeal out of the parking lot. Instead I eased on the accelerator and crept out, careful not to make another scene.

No sooner had I turned onto the highway than my cell phone started ringing. It was Al. I needed to answer though I really, really didn't want to.

"Hello," I said, the irritation in my tone clearly directed toward him. None of this was his fault, though. He was only doing his job. He was a good man, loved God, loved his family, and was extremely loyal. Truth was, I depended on Al and all too often took my frustration out on him. As of late he'd become my whipping boy. Most of the time he just took it with a smile plastered across his face—most of the time.

"What were you thinking, man?" he snapped, frustration in his voice.

"I take it you saw the video?" I replied.

"Me and everyone else," he said. "The church staff has seen it. Lydia Rothschild has seen it!"

"I guess that means she's out?"

"Ya think?"

"Look, Al, we need to nip this thing in the bud, stop it now before it goes too far!"

"Ah . . . it's kind of late for that, Nick."

I switched to my super-positive mode. It amazed me how I could still do that. I had internal switches that I could flip, altering my whole personality based on what performance I needed, what the moment demanded. "Find out what blood-sucker posted it and block it! Get our attorneys on it ASAP! Scare the hell out of whoever did this!"

Al mumbled something that sounded like "teach seminary" under his breath.

"What's that?" I responded. "Speak up, man!"

"I said," he yelled into the phone, "they didn't teach me this in seminary! I didn't sign up for this, Nick. I'm a minister of the gospel, not a—"

I cut him off. "Look, bro, you work for me. Do what I'm telling you!"

"I work for God," he said. "Besides, you don't pay my salary. The church does."

Al was right. It was a ridiculous thing to say. My anger was speaking. I was out of control. I pressed the End Call button and dropped the phone onto the passenger seat.

"You're a real work of art, Nikky boy. You know that?"

"Yeah, I'm aware," I said to the voice in my head, self-hatred pouncing back on me.

I picked the phone back up and called the church.

After several rings someone picked up.

"Hey, Pastor Nick." The voice was calm, soft . . . female.

"Hey, Carla," I said, this time much more kindhearted, maybe a bit pitiful—hitting the switch again. "Look, cancel all my appointments for today and the rest of the week, would you, please? It's been kind of a rough morning."

"Aw," she said empathetically. "I heard. I'm so sorry, Pastor."

"Thank you, Carla."

Driving home, I received a barrage of calls and a string of text messages, all from friends. Most only wanted a piece of me, though. If I wasn't Nick Gregory, they wouldn't give a rat's behind about me. Instead of answering, I muted the volume. Nothing from Abbi, so I assumed she was in flight and would be arriving at Dulles soon enough. Stopped at a red light, I opened one particular text message. It was from a pastor friend in Tulsa—a real man of God I respected, one of the few authentic friends I trusted.

"Nick, I sent you an urgent e-mail. Pease read it."

I whipped into a nearby store parking lot and opened my e-mail. The in-box was crammed full. I scrolled down to Kenny Squires.

Nick,

The strangest thing happened this morning. God woke me up around 2:30 with this crazy sense of urgency to pray for you. I knew you were struggling, but this was like "PRAY FOR NICK NOW!" I fell on my knees next to the bed and cried out to God on your behalf. I wrestled in prayer against the enemy and prayed that God would deliver you from whatever was going on at that moment.

Nick, never forget that despite your past, you belong

to God. The enemy wants to destroy you and your witness. He will lie to you. He will use your past and your mistakes, even your sins to tempt you to give up. The enemy wants to move you into unbelief, but remember you are God's property. Never out of his hands!

God is doing a deep work in you, bringing you to a place in him that you never knew existed. Do not fear. You will emerge from this storm stronger than ever before. Don't give in. Rest in God. Trust his Word. Cling to his promises. They will get you through! Whatever you go through, if you stick with God, in the end he will redeem the mess. Sometimes you have to choose to believe regardless of the circumstances.

Love you, brother! If you need to talk you've got my number.

— Kenny

I remembered how at around 2:30 a.m. I was about to do something very stupid with the pistol when Deuce had been strangely stirred up. Perhaps it was the Holy Spirit? Maybe God was there after all?

I pressed Reply and typed *"Thank you."* That's all I had to offer. After pressing Send I filed the message away.

"That guy's as crazy as you, Nick," the voice taunted. *"He actually thinks God spoke to him! It was just a coincidence. Why would God stop you and not stop Philip?"*

I pulled out of the parking lot and continued driving back home. As I turned onto my street, still a block away from my house, I could see the news crews and protestors gathered around the gates, all waiting for me to arrive, waiting for their shot at Nick Gregory.

7

Not wanting to stop and give the protestors a chance to pounce on me, I pushed the device to open the gate well before reaching the driveway. As my vehicle slowed, they started shouting. Not allowed on my property, they were lined up on the street and sidewalk. There must have been a hundred or so of them, a strange-looking group. What kind of people did this? What did they hope to accomplish? A few brave protesters ventured onto my driveway outside the gate and pounded on the Escalade as it passed them. What could I do? Call the cops, I guess.

"Animal killer!"

"Scumbag!"

"Hypocrite!"

One group had signs. A church group!

"Repent!" one sign read.

"Burn in hell!"

"Nick Gregory is a false prophet!"

I cringed at the hate and venom being spewed. The press stayed at a distance, all too happy to record the protesters. They were masters at making a few people look like a thousand. Eventually, the gate closed behind me and I wove my way up to the house, past the downed camellia bush and the tire ruts in the yard.

"How stupid could you get, Nick?" I mumbled to myself. "You'd better get a grip or you're going to lose everything."

"Too late! It's already over. Ha, ha, ha. You can't turn this around!"

Walking woodenly through the house, it seemed ultrasilent without Abbi's loving and welcoming presence and now without Deuce's. The silence screamed. Passing by Deuce's favorite spot in the kitchen, I noticed the slice of turkey I'd tossed him earlier that morning was gone. He'd eaten it after all. A warm memory flashed across my mind of when he was only a puppy.

* * *

"Deuce, buddy!" I said, dropping my keys on the counter as he came barreling toward me from the great room into the kitchen, his sinewy body sliding sideways on the kitchen floor as he turned a corner. I squatted down and he lunged into my arms, whining, licking me all over.

"*I missed you too, buddy,*" *I said, scratching his head, patting, hugging him tightly.*

"*How was your trip?*" *asked Abbi from the kitchen sink. She was wearing a faded UM sweatshirt with the sleeves pushed up to her elbows. On her hands were yellow scrub gloves. Her auburn hair was pulled back in a ponytail and there was a black smudge on the tip of her nose. She was sweating from all her house-cleaning. From a distance she could have easily passed for a college coed, but up close the slight lines in her face revealed her age. To me, she never looked so beautiful. I put Deuce down and wrapped my arms around her, absorbing her tenderness and scent.*

"*The trip was good,*" *I said, wiping the smudge from her nose,* "*but I missed my wife.*"

"*I missed my husband,*" *she said, pecking me on the lips.*

"*We need to get you a maid.*"

"*Don't be ridiculous.*"

"*You know,*" *I said,* "*it's getting more difficult to be away from you. Three days is about all I can take, if you know what I mean?*"

"*I think I do,*" *she said, pulling off her gloves.* "*The kids won't be home for a couple more hours.*"

Deuce jumped between us. I picked him up and we had a tight group hug.

* * *

I began to feel nauseous and weak. With my clothes still damp, my hand swollen and foot aching, I felt if I stopped moving, everything would collapse and come tumbling down on top of me. While taking a shower, I sat down on the tile bench and pulled the duct tape and blood-soaked paper towel off my foot. I forgot that duct tape rips off hair! The water stung the cut. It could've used a stitch or two. My hand was continuing to throb and swell. I probably fractured it. If it was seriously broken, I reasoned, I'd be out of commission, but going to a doctor right now was out of the question.

Afterward I clicked on the television in the bedroom and tuned it to a cable news channel.

"*New York Times* Best-Selling author and megachurch pastor Nick Gregory is making headlines," the anchorman announced as I wrapped a towel around my body, "amid rumors of a church cover-up involving the death of his son, Philip, marital issues that may include infidelity, and today it appears he deliberately ran over his family dog in a fit of rage." As he spoke, the YouTube video began to play. "I believe this video speaks for itself," he said. When the video clip ended, the scene cut away to me being thronged by reporters as I emerged from the animal clinic and then to the protestors outside the gate of my home.

How could this happen? I thought. *And so fast! People loved me. They couldn't get enough of Nick Gregory. Now they hate me.* I could handle being persecuted for my faith, for standing up for righteousness, but this . . . I was being hated because of my own stupid choices and actions. What was a person supposed to do with that?

"—Our reporter is standing by live at the twenty-thousand-member Grace Life Church," the anchorman was saying. I glanced up as the screen switched to the church.

"I'm here with Al Champion, associate pastor at Grace Life Church," said the blonde reporter.

"What the—" I said, holding my towel around my body.

Al towered over the tiny reporter. A tremendous man, his head and jaw were square and his torso a perfect rectangle. He looked intimidating, but she was unflinching.

"This is yet another blotch on the string of scandals rocking the evangelical world," she said. "Is it any wonder society says that Christians are hypocrites? Borrowing the words of your own, 'What would Jesus do?'"

Al's face lit up as she held out the mic to him. He was in his element. His brows raised and he flashed his million-dollar smile. "Let's get this straight," he said. "Jesus Christ has nothing to do with evil things that happen in this world. There have been many horrible things done in the name of Christ and the church that have nothing to do with the Spirit of Christ." He looked at her and smiled warmly. "The Bible says that we all fall short of the glory of God. That includes me, you, and Nick Gregory. The problem is when people get their eyes off of Jesus and on to fallible men."

Wow, I thought. *Great answer! Way to go, Al.* He clearly had the reporter on the ropes.

"But what about responsibility?" she asked. "Doesn't an

organization that takes in millions of dollars from its members have an obligation to them?"

"Absolutely," said Al, shifting in his stance. "The actions of Pastor Nick are unfortunate," he said, "but they do not reflect this church or our mission. This is unacceptable behavior, and we are taking swift and severe action."

Swift and severe action? I could feel the rage beginning to erupt. *What does that mean? I'll show you "swift and severe"!*

I paused, heart pounding, and took a deep breath to calm myself. *Get a grip. Stay calm. You can't afford another screwup.*

"Is it true," the reporter continued, "there was a cover-up involving Nick Gregory's son?"

"We cannot comment at this time," Al said, "but we are conducting our own internal investigation of the issue. We are prepared to take whatever action is necessary, legal or otherwise."

"What about Abbi Gregory? Rumors are she left your pastor. Why? Has there been infidelity too?"

"Again, no comment," Al said. He looked straight into the camera, smiled large and wide, and said, "Jesus Christ is alive and still offers hope."

Gag me. I clicked off the television, grabbed my cell, and called Al. There was no answer.

Without hesitation, I pressed Call again. Surely Carla would give me the scoop. Again, there was no answer.

8

As much as I hated going back outside, things were unraveling fast. I had to get to the church as quickly as possible and salvage whatever was left of my position, bring some order to the chaos. Despite the shower I still looked like a wreck. Dark circles ringed my bloodshot, sleep-deprived eyes. Unshaven, it seemed I'd gained some gray over the last two weeks, a patch of it this very morning!

Knowing the media was going to be watching my every move, I needed to make myself presentable. I ran a razor over my face and slapped some gel in my hair so it would stick up. This time I dressed professionally yet casually with a cool, relevant look—dress jeans and a black dress shirt with a silver eagle pattern across the back—untucked, of course—and sleeves rolled up to my forearms. After retaping my foot, I carefully slipped on my shiny, black loafers to finish the look.

I grabbed my keys and cell phone one more time and then limped back toward the garage. On the way out, I heard familiar sounds coming from the kitchen—pots and pans. Someone was here. Hope filled my heart. Was Abbi home? Darting into the kitchen, I found . . . Maria, busy cleaning and cooking.

"Maria, what are you doing here?" I asked. "We told you to take a few weeks off until—"

She cut me off. "You need me. Now sit. Breakfast will be ready soon." She was the type of person who didn't take no for an answer.

Thankful for her presence and her kindness, I walked over and kissed her on her forehead. Her silver hair was pulled back, revealing a face weathered and creased from a hard past yet still possessing an inner peaceful glow.

"I'm sorry, Maria," I said, "but I don't have time to eat. I need to get to the church."

"Seems you have plenty of time now," she quipped. Her eyes grew narrow, hands planted on her hips. "You look terrible. When was the last time you ate?"

"Last night."

"What did you eat?"

"What are you now, my mother?" I teased with a slight grin.

"What did you eat?" she repeated.

"Cap'n Crunch," I replied sheepishly.

"Antes de eso?" (Before that?)

"Cap'n Crunch."

"Antes de eso?"

"Peanut butter and jelly," I said. "You happy now? Peanut butter has protein, you know. Besides I haven't had much of an appetite lately."

She clapped her hands and pointed to the chair. *"Siéntese!"*

I obediently dropped into the chair.

"Here, just way you like," she said, serving me a plate of two scrambled eggs with cheese and some homemade salsa poured over the top, with toast and bacon. Then she brought me a bowl of hot oatmeal with cream and a glass of orange juice. "Now eat. You need strength."

My mouth watered as I looked at the splendid display of food set before me. It was obvious the love she put into preparing it. "Why are you doing this?" I asked. She was serving me like a prince but I was feeling like a frog.

"I told you why," she said. Maria's sincerity moved my heart and brought some sanity to the situation. There was something comforting in the simple routine of sitting and eating with another person, someone who cared about me. It caused me to pause and take some deep breaths, to collect myself.

Then the panic set in again. "You don't want to leave me, too, do you?" I shifted uneasily in my seat. "Are you here to collect a check? Is that it? I can write you a check."

She huffed and put her hands on her hips. "I've been paid,"

she said. Patting me on the shoulder, she said, "Señora Abbi made sure of that before she left."

"Abbi told you to look after me, right?"

"No, Señor G," she said, a sadness in her voice, "this has nothing do with her."

I looked up at her. Her eyes were moist.

"I hurt for you and Señora Abbi," she said. "And I know the *real* Señor G that is buried somewhere inside." She tapped me on the chest then wiped her eyes with an apron. *"Ahora coma!"* (Now eat!)

Obediently, I forced a fork full of food in my mouth. After the first bite, I perked up. "Yum. This is good, Maria. You need to get your own cooking show!"

"I've cooked for long time," said Maria. She sat down at the table across from me, reached over, and took my hand in hers. "Listen to this old woman. Go back and find your first love, Señor G," she said then blew a light puff of breath toward me. "Let God breathe his Spirit into your life again and resurrect it. He's still in control." She spoke with authority and wisdom, like someone who'd weathered many storms.

"You've listened to too many of my sermons," I said, downing the glass of orange juice, ignoring the tug on my heart that her words brought.

"You may fool others, but you do not fool me," said Maria, taking the empty glass from my hand and heading to the refrigerator for a refill. "I know you, and this"—she made a circle gesture toward me with her free hand—"is not the real you, the Señor G who gave me hope that someday I will see my husband and my Jesus."

"I hear you, Maria. I really do," I said softly. "I don't know how I got to this point." Pushing away from the table, I had to admit I felt better. Her food was delicious and her words were comforting. Yet, I knew I had to get to the church and fix what could be fixed. So I changed the subject. "Did the media swarm you?"

"*Sí.*"

"I'm sorry."

"No worries," she said. "I told them, 'Why do you not report on good news like the thousands of orphans Grace Life Church feeds, clothes, and educates? You forget that big earthquake in Los Angeles, *sí?* Grace Life led a major relief effort that helped my relatives. Why do you not report on the lives turned around—the homeless taken off the street, babies saved, marriages restored, crippled healed, souls brought to Christ? *Alabado Dios!* (Praise God!) If any of you were in Señor G's position there'd be so much trash on you, they'd have to bring in a garbage truck!"

I chuckled. "You told them that?"

"Oh, *sí!*" She flipped her dish towel over her shoulder.

"You are good. Sure glad you're on my side!"

Maria smiled, wiping her hands on the dish towel.

"Have you heard from Abbi?" I asked her.

"No, señor."

"I sure miss her."

"Me too."

"You haven't mentioned Deuce," I said. "You know what happened?"

Maria nodded.

"You know it was an accident, right?"

She looked at me with a *what-a-stupid-question-that-was* expression. "I know how much you love that dog," she said. "He's going to be fine. I sense it in my spirit."

"Really? And do you sense anything about Abbi?" I asked.

She shifted her eyes to the table and picked up my dirty plates. "You need to go now," she said.

"Thank you, Maria," I said, giving her a hug. "Hey, one more thing. My office is a mess. Please don't clean it, okay? I mean it. I want it left alone."

"*No problemo,*" she said with a wink.

My cell vibrated indicating a call. Turning the ringer volume back up, I looked at the caller. This time it was Martin Nichols, head of our church board. I let it go to voice mail then listened to his message.

"Nick, you need to come in now. It's urgent. Security is here to help you get through the crowd."

About the time I finished listening, he sent a text repeating his voice message.

I texted back "*K*" and pushed Send.

9

The sky still overcast and dreary, a steady drizzle was falling. Backing out of the garage for the second time that morning, this time slower and more carefully, I was fully aware of
the eyes fixed on me from the street. After turning around, I
headed forward down the drive. When I was about halfway
down, a good seventy-five feet past the downed camellia bush,
a sheriff's patrol car pulled up to the closed gate. The second
his car stopped, the media swarmed around the vehicle like
an army of ants. It gave me a warped bit of satisfaction to see
them struggling under their umbrellas to keep themselves and
their equipment dry. He just sat there patiently, ignoring them.
Seeing me coming toward him, he motioned for me to let him
in. I pushed the remote to open the gate then backed up into
the driveway turnaround and waited, putting as much distance

as possible between the crowd and my car. Easing his patrol car up next to mine, the sheriff motioned for me to come to his window and then looked down, apparently reading his computer. I stuck my umbrella out the door, popped it open, and walked over. Thunder clapped in the distance, but there was no lightning.

Peering up from his computer, the sheriff showed no emotion and looked directly at me. "Are you Nick Gregory?"

"That would be me," I answered.

"I'm Sheriff Gilroy. I heard you've had a pretty rough morning," he said, with a tone of unexpected compassion.

"Yep," I said, "pretty rough. What's this about? You here to arrest me for running over my dog?"

"Well, not exactly," he said with a slight grimace, "but I'm afraid this isn't going to make things any better." At that, he handed me an official envelope through the open window. "You've been served."

My lips twisted and forehead crunched as I took the envelope.

"Sorry," he said. "I have to say that, you know."

"It's all right. You're only doing your job."

"Yes sir," he said, holding out a clipboard with a delivery confirmation for me to sign.

I'm not left-handed, so I scribbled my name the best I could with my injured hand. Just trying to grip the pen made my knuckles sting.

"Mr. Gregory," he said. "I know this is probably not the

best time, but I wanted to tell you that I read your book *Peak to Peak: The Secrets of Mountaintop Living.* It helped me through a tough spot. I don't read much. A friend gave it to me and I tossed it in the backseat and forgot about it. Then one night sitting in the patrol car, I got desperate and remembered it was back there. I picked it up and read all night—couldn't stop. It came at just the right time, one of those God things you talk about. I've got it right here." He thrust the book through his window. "Would it be asking too much for you to sign it? I see your hand is hurt."

"I think I can manage," I said. "You guys are doing a great work." I tried to think of some clever line to write inside his book, but because my hand was sore, I just quickly scribbled my name again and handed it back. "Glad the book helped," I said.

"I appreciate it," he replied. "And just so you know, I don't believe everything I hear. Stand strong, my friend."

"Thanks," I said. *If only the rumors weren't true.*

He nodded politely and started backing down the drive.

It didn't take a rocket scientist to know what was inside the envelope. Though I had hoped against hope, prayed, and begged, I knew in my gut it was only a matter of time. Still, nothing prepares a man for such news. What was funny, I thought, as I got back into the Escalade and started reading the words on the summons, was that I couldn't even cry. I was just too numb.

IN THE DISTRICT COURT OF FAIRFAX COUNTY, VIRGINIA

In the Matter of the Marriage of:

Abigail H. Gregory versus **Nick T. Gregory**

My eyes skimmed the document.

Nick T. Gregory (hereafter called the DEFENDANT)

Abigail H. Gregory (hereafter called the PLAINTIFF)

"Is that what we've been reduced to, Abbi?" I whispered.

I let the papers fall into my lap. I couldn't read any further, not now. Just when I thought my day couldn't get any more absurd, I got served divorce papers! I knew one thing for sure. Abbi felt betrayed and angry. She was furious. She should be. She had placed absolute trust in God and in me.

In our marriage, our ministry, we'd been such a team—a partnership from the beginning. I guess when someone loves and trusts as deeply as Abbi did, the level of hurt and betrayal was off the charts. No telling what she would do when she found out about Deuce. I slipped the papers back into the envelope and drove out the gate through the throng of reporters.

What next? Could this day get any worse? I had a feeling in my gut that it was about to.

"Hey, Nikky boy! I told you. God didn't answer your prayers.

He let you down again. He must be deaf! Remember how hard you cried out to him to bring Abbi back? Ha! What do you think about your God now? I told you. He's not there! He didn't show up. Wait till she finds out about Deuce!"

10

The church scene was crazy.

Reporters swarmed like a hive of stirred-up bees—CNN, FOX, CBS, ABC, NBC, CBN—all the big ones. Someone had tipped them off that I was coming. As I eased into my parking space in front of our forty-million-dollar facility, my mind flashed back to some twenty years earlier when we were meeting in a rented warehouse with only a handful of people. I was a part-time seminary student struggling to get the church planted and Abbi worked as a bank teller to help ends meet. Times were lean, but we were a team full of vision, on fire and determined to make an impact for Christ. I glanced around at the news crews scurrying around my vehicle. This was certainly not the kind of impact we had envisioned.

I killed the engine and sat there. A sinking, lonely sensation gnarled in the pit of my stomach. The ache I was experiencing in my hand and foot paled in comparison to the mountain of wrong that was accusing me—Philip, Deuce, Abbi. Glancing over at the divorce papers on the seat I thought, *I can't believe she actually went through with it.* I was holding out for an absurd miracle that she would want me back.

Just as Martin had promised, security was waiting to escort me from the vehicle into the building. The tension in the air slapped me hard as I stepped through the conference room door. It felt more like an intervention than a board meeting. There were thirteen of them including Al, who was the only non–board member present—eleven men and two women. My eyes scanned the group sitting around the table, a variety of emotions painted on their faces—anger, hurt, disappointment, shock, and sadness. One of the women members refused to meet my gaze and dabbed her eyes with a tissue. *How many wonderful projects have been planned, prayed over, and birthed around this very table?* I thought. *Sure didn't plan on birthing this.*

Like Al, these were all good people, men and women of strong faith and wisdom who'd come alongside me to do ministry and build the church. They'd been carefully selected and approved by our elders, our staff pastors, the church body, and finally me. Several had been with Grace Life from its inception. They'd made supreme sacrifices of time, effort, and money. One of our board members, a tech executive, had turned down a lucrative job offer that would have relocated him to the West

Coast. When he didn't go, I asked him why. "God called me to serve here," he explained. "When I prayed for direction, God didn't release me to go." That's the kind of dedicated, God-loving people who served on our board. They weren't "yes" men (and women); they were Holy Spirit–led and carefully chosen. I loved these people, counted on them. That being said, the emotions today had nothing to do with warm memories and camaraderie. We'd intentionally set up the board so I would have limited power—for times just like this, so a single person could not override the board. None of us gave this clause much thought because of the remote possibility of ever having to invoke it.

"Okay, we're all here," said Martin Nichols, a tall, lean man with salt-and-pepper hair. A runner in his early sixties, he shut the door behind me.

"What's this about?" I asked awkwardly, defensively. A stupid question, I know.

"Please sit down, Nick," Martin said cordially. I limped to the end of the table, cradling my sore hand, and pulled up a chair.

"You look like you need a doctor," said one of the men.

"I'm fine," I lied.

Al sat at the opposite end of the table from me.

"Sharon," Martin said, still standing. "Would you please open us in prayer?"

"Yes," said Sharon. She bowed her head and began praying as if heaven itself depended on her ability to articulate the right words. "Father God, you know all things. Nothing takes you by surprise. You know why we are gathered here, and we ask for your divine wisdom in this situation."

Everyone had bowed their heads and closed their eyes except Al and me. His eyes locked with mine for a couple of seconds before he closed them.

Sharon continued her prayer. "Let your spirit of peace rest on us today. Above all else, we seek to bring you glory. Amen."

"Thank you, Sharon," said Martin, sitting down at the table. He turned his attention to me. "Nick, we all know what's going on here. There's no easy way to say this. It pains all of us here because we love you and know how much you are suffering right now. You've been used of God mightily. But the fact is, you are emotionally unstable and in no condition to pastor. You need to step down."

"I take it this is your 'swift and severe action'?" I said defensively.

"You need to step down and focus your full attention on restoring your marriage and getting yourself healed."

Another kick in the gut. "My marriage?" I replied. "I thought this was about the video."

"It's a combination of things that have been building," said Martin. "Abbi informed us of her intentions, and then your rampage on the video—that was the last straw."

My heart sank. "Uh . . . still, don't you think this is a bit harsh? I mean, sure, things are a little crazy right now. What about a leave of absence while I work things out? That's the normal process. I mean, come on, I've been the senior pastor for twenty years. I started this church, remember?"

"These are extraordinary circumstances, Nick," said Martin. "We feel if you just take a leave of absence you'll still see yourself as pastor and have your hand in the church affairs, which will distract your focus from your marriage and your personal healing."

Knowing there was no good way out of the hole I had dug, I dropped my head down into my folded arms on the table.

"The press has been digging around for anything they can get on us. Rumors are circulating about Philip and why Abbi is leaving you. There's going to be a full investigation. And now this dog video. It's only been a few hours, Nick, and it's already getting national attention. The media is foaming at the mouth for a scandal. This is going to be big. If we act now we can maybe slow it down and minimize the damage to the church. You stepping down would be for the greater good."

"Maybe good for you, I'm the scapegoat," I said.

"Now, Nick, you know perfectly well this is not the first time we've talked to you about your escalating destructive behavior. This has been going on for some time. The complaints have been increasing while the numbers and offerings have been steadily decreasing. The church simply can't afford for you to continue in a leadership role."

"You can't do this," I protested, grasping at straws. "We have a protocol. It has to go through the elders and then a church vote."

"Yes, we can, Nick," said Martin. "Besides, you don't want to go through that process. Trust me. It'll be messy." He turned his attention to another board member. "John, read him Section 13.c of our bylaws."

John began to read. "Section 13.c . . . In the event of extraordinary circumstances such as—"

"Stop it!" I shouted, standing to my feet. "Okay! I get it! You can have your stinking church!"

"God loves you, Nick," said one of the women. "We love you too. It's not like we're throwing you to the wolves. We've given you lots of chances. You need healing and counseling. We're prepared to walk through this journey with you. We support you."

"Great—thanks for your support! No, you're not throwing me to the wolves!" I laughed, deep and cynical. "You *are* the wolves! Look, I built this church! You wouldn't even be here if it weren't for me!" No one spoke as I finished my tirade. "So, what's the deal? Who's taking my place? Tell me that."

Al cleared his throat. I turned to him, rage in my eyes. "How could you? All that talk about love and service. You've been waiting to make your move, take my position!"

"That's not true, Nick!" said Al. "I'm grieved over this. This whole ordeal breaks my heart and God's too. But something has to be done. I'm trusting that God's in control. I believe he can use this situation to bring you closer to him and to use this ultimately for his good will and purpose."

"You're so holy, Al," I sneered. "Good for you." I paused,

massaged the bridge of my nose with my thumb and index finger, let my eyes close a moment then opened them.

Feeling the hurt and sting of betrayal, my thoughts
turned to Abbi and how she must feel at my betrayal of her.
This was why she had lashed out at me so venomously. Pain
causes people to do that. Turning to Al I said, "What about
when you told me that your only call from God was to support
and stand beside me?"

Al didn't respond, only stared calmly ahead. I could tell it
pained him to hear my pathetic rant, but that didn't slow me
down.

"And love!" I shouted to all thirteen of them. "Don't talk to
me about love! You're a pack of opportunistic wolves! Wolves
in sheeps' clothing!"

"We're not the one who ran down the dog," said one of
them. "You're out of control, Nick."

My eyes scanned the group around the table staring up at
me with concern, but I knew they were judging me. "I can't
take any more of this!" I shouted. "I'm out of here!"

11

Exploding recklessly out of the conference room, I limped as briskly as I could down the hallway. Turning a corner, I collided head-on with Jamison, one of our maintenance men, who was carrying a drill and a box of screws. He flew backward and screws went everywhere. Really? Again? This was getting ridiculous. Hope this doesn't make it on YouTube too! I can see the headlines now. "Pastor Nick runs down innocent church worker!" I was expecting him to yell at me or something worse, but Jamison only looked up with eyes full of compassion, like Deuce, like Maria, like Kenny Squires. I reached out with my good hand to grasp his and help him to his feet. He gripped me firmly and I pulled him up.

"Pastor," he said gently, still holding my hand, squeezing, "all of this is not you. I know the real you. You led me to Jesus when I was hopeless. He changed my life. He's alive! Only God could change me. Do you remember the mess I was? The addict I was?"

"I remember," I said.

"God delivered me and used you to bring me the message of hope."

"He sure did."

"It was a miracle. This church took me in off the street— got me help. Gave me this job. You taught me the truth." Jamison put his arms around me and squeezed. "Thank you, Pastor Nick," he said. "My heart is breaking for you."

"Mine's breaking, too, Jamison." I pulled away from his embrace and looked him squarely in the eyes. "Whatever happens to me, never give up on God. We're all in need of his constant grace. We all fall short, even me. You hear?"

"Yes sir. I do."

"Good," I said and continued down the corridor.

I was about to blast through the door leading outside to the parking lot, when someone shouted at me.

"Nick, wait!" It was Al. He was jogging toward me.

I ignored him and kept walking. "Why should I wait for you?" I yelled back.

"Just wait, please!"

I stopped and let him catch up. "What?" I snapped.

"Look," he said, huffing for breath, "I'm sorry."

"You're out of shape is what you are."

"This wasn't my idea, Nick. It was a board decision."

I stared defiantly at him and through clenched jaws said, "I'm sure you fought really hard for me."

"It's the right thing and you know it," he said, placing his hand on my shoulder. "I'm praying for you, Nick."

"You do that, Al," I said, jerking away and then shooting out the door.

Outside, sunshine slammed me in the face, causing me to squint. The rain had finally stopped and security was waiting to escort me to my car. Reporters surrounded the Escalade, blocking the doors. One of my security detail stepped in front of me. "I'm going to have to ask you to step aside," he told them. The reporters parted like the Red Sea.

"What about the dog?" a reporter shouted.

"It was an unfortunate accident," I said.

"It didn't look like an accident."

"Is he going to live?"

"I hope so."

"What about the alleged cover-up involving your son, Philip? Was that an accident too?"

Ignoring the question, I opened the door to my vehicle and slid inside. This time I couldn't get out of the parking lot fast enough. About the time I turned onto the highway, my cell phone rang again. I looked down and saw the call was from Carlee. My precious Carlee. In the commotion of the morning, I'd forgotten all about her. Tenderhearted, passionate about the things of God, she was studying nursing at the University of Maryland. It was her last year, but she was planning on continuing for her master's degree and had been looking into other programs around the country. Philip's death had been hard on her, but her faith was resilient. It was difficult watching my baby girl struggle through some tough issues. I gripped the wheel with my left hand, blew out a slow stream of air, and answered the phone with my injured right hand.

"Hello, sweetheart," I answered in a calm voice.

"Daddy!" Carlee cried into the phone, bursting into sobs. "How could you?"

"Oh, honey," I moaned. "I'm so sorry."

"Deuce, Daddy! Deuce!" she shouted. "Is he dead?"

"I don't think so."

"First it was Philip! Now Deuce! You're an embarrassment. Everybody is looking at me like I have a disease or something. How can I to go to class? I feel like hiding. I wish you never were my dad! Mom was right!"

"Carlee, I—"

Click.

At that point, the blackest, darkest cloud of depression I had ever experienced descended upon me, smothering my mind, even more so than earlier that morning in bed with the pistol. Having Carlee call me out was worse than a thousand accusing board meetings. I was her hero, or maybe I used to be, and now I had broken her heart too. This was the all-time low. I could feel myself being sucked deeper and deeper into the nightmarish black hole of despair.

"You're garbage, Nick. You're nothing! You hear me? Nothing!

Your ambition killed your son. Abbi's divorcing you because you betrayed her. Carlee will never forgive you. The world hates you now. You're a laughingstock. You'll never write or preach again. I told you everything was coming down. You deserve to die."

Panic seized me again, and my chest felt as though it was in that wrenching vise.

Sweating.

Shaking.

Choking.

Drowning, gasping for breath.

"God!" That was it. My prayers had been boiled down to that one word.

"You deserve to die, Nick. Your son is dead, and your wife and daughter hate you. What's the use of going on?"

Merging onto the interstate, my mind glazed over and I felt the autopilot kick in again. *"Philip had the guts!"* I quickly sped up to 75 mph, then to 85. Swerving into the left lane, I passed a string of cars and trucks and came up behind a car only going 80. I tailgated until he moved over into the right lane. After passing several more sets of traffic, pushing three more creepers into the slower lane, I could see open road, at least for a while. *"Philip had the guts!"*

At that point everything became a blur. I have no idea how fast I was driving. Bridges, vehicles, and highway signs flashed past me with lightning speed. Blue flashing lights appeared in my rearview mirror. Instead of slowing down, I slammed down on the accelerator. Then I saw it. The spot was coming into view. I knew it well. *"Philip had the guts! Philip had the guts, you coward!"* I decided to end it all—right there.

Wanting to make it look like an accident, I started texting. "Hey, Al," I typed as I unbuckled my seat belt, turned the Escalade's steering wheel, and headed toward the concrete piling. *"You're crazy, Nick! God will surely forgive you. If he's not real, then it'll be sweet oblivion. Philip had the guts!"* At the last moment, I screamed, "God, please stop me!" There was no way I'd survive this. I was doing my family a favor.

I felt nothing, not even pain. My spirit didn't float out of my body, nor did I hover over the scene of the accident. I didn't watch the paramedics as they used the Jaws of Life to extract my mangled body from the wreckage. There was no tunnel. No white light. Everything went black.

12

The first thing I felt was the heat, unbearable heat, stinging my skin. It was warm and humid in D.C., but not excru-
ciatingly hot like this. Slowly, I cracked open my eyes then
instantly slammed them shut again. The light . . . the light was
so bright it burned my eyes. Squinting didn't help.

Shielding my eyes with my hand, I blinked them open
again, just barely. Nothing but light shone all around, nothing
but blinding, burning light. I tried to swallow, but my throat
was parched and raw, lips chapped and blistered. Obviously, I
was alive because my whole body throbbed in agony. And the
smell! Putrid! I gagged and coughed. Yes, my senses were fully
awake and I was still very much breathing. But where was I?

I knew one thing for sure. I was not in *the* light—not *that*
light. One was supposed to experience overwhelming love,

peace, an absence of pain, and hear glorious music in *that* light—not burning, searing, pain—not aching in the legs and chest. But if not in *that* light, then where was I? I considered the alternative. *Was I in hell? No, couldn't be . . . Hell doesn't have light. Or does it?* At least my theology never gave room for that. Hell was a place void of *the* light, total darkness, complete absence of God. The Bible speaks of flames, of the lake of fire. I guess that gives off some light. Wherever I was, it was hot, definitely hot, and the odor was repulsive.

Regret seized me. Fear engulfed me. A sickening nausea rose up in the pit of my stomach. *What have you done, Nick?* I thought. *You idiot!* I rolled over facedown, prostrate in the scorching light, waiting for some higher power to speak.

"God," I whispered, "I messed up. I was out of my mind, not thinking straight. Please have mercy on me. I'm so sorry."

Something was in my mouth!

"Ugh!" I spat. Dirt! It was gritty dirt! I coughed and spat again, wiping my chapped and blistered lips. With my stomach flat on the ground, I did a half push-up lifting my head to look down at the ground. The light shone around me and underneath me, illuminating the barren ground below my face.

Dirt.

Sand.

Rocks.

Lots of rocks. Pitted rocks. Rolling on my side, I cupped my hand over my eyes shielding them from the . . . yes, from the sun. That was it! The light intensely raging down on me was the scorching sun! What a relief. That meant I wasn't dead! I was alive! *I must have been thrown from the Escalade.*

Still groggy and disoriented, I squinted through the blinding sunlight trying to make sense of the terrain and my current condition. Several huge boulders jutted up around me, and there were what appeared to be mountains close by. *Strange,* I thought, *D.C. doesn't have mountains . . . or boulders. And where'd all the trees go . . . and the people? This place seems more like the moon or Mars.*

Rumbling in the distance caught my attention, jerking me back to the present.

A vehicle.

The sound became louder, closer. *A nearby road perhaps?* I pulled myself up in the sitting position and turned toward the increasing sound. There was no road in sight, yet I noticed a vehicle with one blinding headlight about a half mile away thundering directly toward me at a high rate of speed, dust whipping up behind it, waves of heat rising from the sandblasted and wasted earth. Because the brilliance of the headlight was blinding me, I couldn't make out the type of vehicle. My first thought was a motorcycle, a big one like a Harley-Davidson. It's common for them to have a huge single round headlight on in the day. As it drew closer, however, I realized the light wasn't a headlight at all, but the sun reflecting off a silver or chrome piece of armor or shield of some sort. And the rumbling wasn't an engine but the sound of horses' hooves! The sun was reflecting off the front of a silver and bronze chariot wagon–looking thing being pulled by two horses.

A chariot?

Yes, it was a chariot with a canvas-tarp kind of top protecting the two men riding in it from the blazing sun.

"What the—?"

Instinctively, without thinking, like something else was controlling my body, I dropped flat and rolled behind one of the nearby boulders. *Weird,* I thought. *Why'd I do that?* Before I could even process what was happening, the chariot had stopped in front of the giant rock I was behind and the driver began shouting at me in a foreign language. "מכאן אתה כלב מטונף יצא!" *(Get out here, you filthy dog!)* he ordered.

The man screaming insults at me was odd, to say the least. Clad in tunic and sandals, his balding head was disproportionally large for his neck and body. Face scrunched up as if he'd been sucking sour lemons, his eyebrows were sinister and bushy, nose long and crooked. I recognized that he was speaking an ancient dialect of Hebrew. But what was even stranger was the fact that I understood him perfectly! I'd studied Hebrew in seminary, but only enough to do word studies. Yet, somehow, I comprehended his humiliating order as if it were spoken in English!

Next to the skinny guy with the big head was the driver of the chariot, a giant of a man wearing silver military armor and leather girths. He wore a silver armband up around his bulging bicep with the words *House of David* engraved on it—in

Hebrew, of course. An intimidating figure, his jaw was locked and his muscles ripped. He was big, but clearly not the one in charge. He reminded me a lot of Al Champion.

"It's time!" yelled the skinny guy with the big head again, his words still in Hebrew. "You knew this day would eventually come. Did you really think I wouldn't find you?" He let out a grating, cynical laugh. "How'd you get out here this far away from everybody?"

"I don't know," I responded, still sitting in the dirt, looking up. But instead of English, the words that floated out of my mouth were in ancient Hebrew, as if it were my native tongue! *Okay, this is really crazy.* "Last thing I remember," I continued in Hebrew, "I was in my Escalade when I . . . it slammed into a concrete pylon."

"Your what?" he asked, face all contorted and confused. "What's an Escalade?"

"What's concrete?" said the big guy next to him.

"You're serious, aren't you?" I said. They continued to stare at me like I was some sort of alien from another planet. Maybe I was.

An eerie sensation came over me, like I was in danger, so I tried leaping to my feet to get out of there, but my legs wouldn't budge. Falling flat, my face slammed into the stony ground with a hard thud, the jagged rocks digging into my palms and knees. I cried out in agony while the two men broke out in mocking laughter. Blood, mingled with salt and grit, trickled over my blistered lips, stinging them. It was when I touched the back of my hand to my lip that I saw them. Why hadn't I noticed them before? I guess I was too caught up in my strange surroundings to notice.

My hands.

They were repulsive. Hairy and encrusted from neglect, the fingernails were long and curled, turning green from fungus growing under them as if they belonged to some old troll that lived under a bridge. These were not my hands. I held up my right one, the injured one, and examined it. Nothing swollen or sprained—it was *not* the same hand that had punched the wall early that morning.

And my legs.

Twisted, crushed, and broken.

Strangely, like everything else in this world, as I felt them, I noticed they were old breaks that had healed that way. Apparently, they were wounds that had occurred years before. They couldn't have come from the crash, impossible. There was no blood and no fresh lacerations. And I was wearing some kind of dirty tunic and crude sandals just like Baldy in the chariot. My toenails were creepy too!

The Escalade! Where is it? I rotated my crooked body around, scanning the area again. My vehicle was nowhere in sight, only stony mountains with caves and the flat, barren desert stretching for miles and miles.

"What are you looking for, another cave to hide in?" Big Mouth asked. "There's no escape. Now get up, I said!"

"What do you want with me?" I demanded, pulling myself

up on my elbows. A strong breeze whipped the hot air, stinging my eyes and stirring up that putrid smell. "Ugh! What's that smell?" I asked. "Your horses?"

The two men roared with laughter. "That's you, you nasty dog! When's the last time you bathed? Before your nurse dropped you off that wall?" They doubled over in shameless laughter, ridiculing. "If Saul and Jonathan were alive to see you now they'd be disappointed. You know why? Because you're a worthless dog, Mephibosheth!"

Mephibosheth? I remembered that name. Yes, from seminary. I even wrote a paper on him. Got an A+. I still could remember the first lines I wrote of the paper. "Mephibosheth—a peculiar crippled man whose story is tucked away, almost hidden, in the vast archives of the Old Testament."

"Hey, wait a minute!" I shouted back while looking up at my accusers from the parched landscape. "I'm not Mephibosheth! My name is Nick . . . Nick Gregory! I'm a pastor from Washington, D.C. I write books. I crashed my SUV."

They looked at each other like cows staring at a new gate. "Washington? Where's that?" They both cracked up again. "Is that in the Philistine camp?"

"Certainly not," I said then looked down at my miserable self. "It's . . . Oh, never mind. You wouldn't understand."

"Come on, Mephibosheth! What do you take us for, uncircumcised Hivites? Everybody knows you've been living in Machir's house over in Lo-debar for the past twentysomething years! You think you've been safely hiding out, but the truth is, nobody cared enough to search you out because they heard how disgusting you are! They didn't want to find you. You're a living dead man!"

"I'm not Mephibosheth!" I shouted, spitting out a mixture of blood and grit. "I am Nick Gregory!"

"Okay, Nick," Big Head said. "Whatever you say. Why did you leave Machir's house and make me come all the way out in this godforsaken desert to search for you?" Exasperated, he raised his arms and then let them drop. "You know there's no water on this side of the mountain. How'd you get out here anyway? I know you didn't crawl. That would've taken days. You'd be dead already! How long did you think you'd last out here? Did you think I wouldn't find you?"

"I didn't crawl." I heard myself speak, but it felt like I was outside my own body. *Whoa. Where did that come from? Did I just say that?* It was my mouth, but not my words. Just like when I rolled behind the boulder earlier and it wasn't me, the words were Mephibosheth's. *This is crazy!*

"When I heard you were coming for me," said Mephibosheth through my mouth, "I paid Zeripan to bring me. I was hoping to be dead before you found me. I would rather die out here alone than at the king's hand. I am worthless, as you say. Please, just let me die in peace."

The man with the big head let out another menacing laugh. All the laughing was really starting to grate on my nerves.

I scratched Mephibosheth's head, remembering my seminary paper. "Hey, that means you must be Ziba," I said.

He looked at me as if I'd lost my mind. "Well, give the guy some spelt and honey! He knows my name."

I struggled to my feet, leaning wobbily on the crude crutches that were as crooked as my legs. Carved out of tree branches, the shoulder pad on each one was a clump of nasty rags. When I finally stood, I caught a glimpse of my reflection, or Mephibosheth's reflection, in the chariot's shield. My—his face was worse than the unkempt hands and feet—gross, half-rotted teeth; dirty, scaly skin, with sores; knotted hair; and a crusty beard. Stunned at who I'd become, I recoiled in disgust.

"Gaius," Ziba said to his massive companion. "Make him drink!" Then Ziba turned back to me. "You're not dying on me, Mephibosheth. Not on my watch! The king wants to see you, and I'm going to deliver."

13

Gaius stepped down from the chariot and walked toward me. He wasn't quite Goliath, but he was big, really big. Because of Mephibosheth's crooked body, my head came to around his pecs. The polar opposite of Ziba, Gaius had a lot of hair. His long, flowing black locks fell below his shoulders, matching his black beard. The more I thought about it, he could have just as easily been Samson or Russell Crowe.

"Drink!" Gaius ordered in Hebrew, shoving in my face a canteen that looked like it was made out of some type of animal skin.

Mephibosheth might have wanted to die out here in the desert, but I was thirsty! I took a long, deep gulp, water trickling down my beard and neck. "Ahh," I said, wiping my mouth with my forearm.

"You sure don't drink like a guy wanting to die!" said Ziba.

I cut him with my eyes and handed the canteen back to Gaius.

"Pick him up and let's get out of here," ordered Ziba and Gaius reached down to pick me up.

"I got this," I snapped, or Mephibosheth snapped. Like I said, it was weird. It was like a blending of our minds was taking place. In some bizarre, supernatural way we were linked. I knew Mephibosheth's thoughts, his history. While I could still remember it, the other world that I came from seemed more like a dream now, a dream that was fading. I was still me, Nick Gregory, with all my emotions, yet I was Mephibosheth too.

Ziba stepped aside as I slowly hobbled toward the chariot. Both feet were lame, but one worked better than the other one, which dragged the ground behind me, making a trail in the dirt. The two of them stared at each other and waited . . . and waited . . . and waited. Gaius fiddled with the horse's bridles and gave them a drink from some larger water skins that were being carried in the back of the chariot. While waiting, the two men talked about me as if I wasn't even there.

"Can you believe the king sent for him?" said Ziba.

"I don't get it," said Gaius. "He can't work or fight. I mean, what good is he?"

"I hear you," said Ziba. "All I know is I was brought before the king and asked if there was still someone still living from Saul's house. I said, 'Yeah, but he's a guy crippled in both feet.' Next thing you know, he wants me to go get him. I never thought the king would take me seriously."

Mephibosheth's crutch hit a stone, twisted, and he fell flat again.

"Mephibosheth! Come on!" Ziba shouted. "Our supply of water is going to be dried up by the time you get here!"

I struggled to my feet and continued the final few yards.

At the chariot, I assessed the situation closer. It was like a chariot version of a pickup truck with a mat in the back for Mephibosheth. Awkwardly, I placed my crutches in the back then gripped the railing and attempted to pull myself up. Like doing pull-ups, the weight of Mephibosheth's whole body bore down on my arms. Trying to swing his torso up and over, I only made it about halfway up before slamming into the side of the chariot. Falling back, I hit the hard, dusty ground with a thud, landing on rocks . . . again. I lay there, humiliated, in the scorching heat, my head spinning.

"Please, Ziba, curse me," I said as Mephibosheth. "Leave me and let me die! God has cursed me. I'm worthless."

"I told you," replied Ziba. "The king wants to see you. Why? I have no idea. But you are right. You are worthless. I pity you."

With that, Gaius lifted me up and sat me down in the back of the chariot. As he did, I had a fuzzy memory of gathering Deuce in my own arms. I wondered how he was doing. How long ago was it? Was he even alive? Was I in some kind of parallel universe?

"Why are you so cruel to me?" I asked Ziba as my arm accidentally brushed his shoulder.

"Because you make my life difficult," he said. "And do *not* touch me, you filthy dog!"

I should be the one telling you what to do, Ziba! I thought as Mephibosheth. *There's no justice in this world, or I wouldn't be like this.* Snarling like the dog I was, I slid down in the back of the chariot and curled up in a ball.

The journey from the desert wasteland of Lo-debar to Jerusalem was a taxing trek. As Nick, I could just hop in an air-conditioned vehicle, pipe up the stereo, and be there in about four hours. A jet could get me there in less than one. But this wasn't 2015. It was 1000 BC.

Don't get me wrong; our chariot was clipping along pretty good. The horses maintained a steady gait despite the harsh and unforgiving landscape. Up, down, and across the rocky mountain terrain, I gained a new respect for the guy who invented shock absorbers! Not designed for comfort, the chariot didn't have much of a suspension system, if any. When the bronze and wooden wheels rolled down the path, I felt every pebble, rock, and pothole, my head jostling around like a bobble-head doll.

It was unbearably hot and arid, and my nose felt raw from breathing in and swallowing dusty grit kicked up by the horses. I wrapped a coarse scarf around my head, allowing only for my eyes. At times, the dust whipping up was so bad I covered them too.

Curled up in the back of the chariot, I listened to Ziba and Gaius go on and on about King David's military conquests and all the latest happenings in Jerusalem that they referred to as the House of David. Sitting there, I thought about all the historians and scholars, my professors in seminary and pastor friends who'd give an arm and a leg (no pun intended) to be in my position, actually participating in ancient biblical history.

14

Miserable, I pulled my crippled legs to my chest, trying to stay as still as possible and endure the ride. Being stuck in the back of a chariot for a couple of days in the blistering, suffocating heat in another dude's messed-up body will give a guy some time to think. What was I doing here? Was this some kind of hallucination or reverse reincarnation? Was I being punished? I knew reincarnation wasn't biblical, but this was miserable and it wasn't a dream. It was real flesh and blood, real pain. Could I be dead? Is this some level of hell? Maybe this is a type of purgatory? I'd always taught the idea of purgatory was thoroughly unbiblical. I still believed it was unbiblical. Die once, face God's judgment. If so, where was I and how did I get into Mephibosheth's body? How come he had control? It was like I was trapped, forced to participate in a scenario I had no desire to be in.

Recalling my seminary paper on Mephibosheth, it was one of my best. My professor had even written across the page, underneath the big A+, *"Nick, your writing is crisp and alive. Good argumentation and smooth writing style. You use good imagery and such theological balance. Excellent variety in paragraph and sentence construction. It vivifies your writing and holds the reader's attention."* Coming from one of the toughest seminary professors, those words were like gasoline on sparks. I'd gone over them so many times they'd become etched in my memory. I knew writing would be a part of my future. Looking back, why had I chosen that particular story to write about? Was there some connection to me being here now? I knew who Ziba was. I knew the story.

The bumpy journey, jolting my body around, was finally getting to me. Something rumbled inside me. *You've got to be kidding.* I tried to ignore it, but the rumbling intensified into cramps. I sat up holding my stomach, rocking back and forth. Twisting around, I took Mephibosheth's bony finger, its nails overgrown and curling, and tapped Ziba on the shoulder. "Hey, man," I said in Hebrew. "Ah . . . excuse me."

He recoiled back away from me like a cobra then whipped around, glaring. "Don't touch me, you dog!" he hissed. "What do you want now?"

Man, have you got issues. And enough with the dog trip already.

"I have to . . . you know," I said, motioning below my waistline, "go."

Ziba rolled his eyes and slapped the top of his tremendous head.

I shrugged my shoulders. "Hey, when you gotta go, you gotta go."

"Stop the horses!" he ordered Gaius, who pulled the reins, bringing the chariot to a halt. After the dust settled, both of them stared at me and waited.

I looked around on all sides. On one side of the chariot was desert, not a single palm tree in sight, nothing but heat waves rising up from the drought-stricken ground. On the other side, stony mountains stood a good distance away, a couple of miles at least. There were some larger boulders within walking distance—for a normal guy, that is. I struggled to lift my body, but my legs wouldn't cooperate. I tugged on one leg with my hands, then on the other. The process was painfully slow and the progress minimal.

"Oh, for the love of Melchizedek!" said Ziba. "Gaius, pick him up!"

Hulk got down from the chariot, reached into the back, and picked me up with my crutches. A few paces from the chariot, he just dropped me in open space. I wobbled to my feet once more and stood there supporting myself with the crutches. The two men just looked at me, waiting. It seemed people waited a lot for Mephibosheth.

"Squat!" shouted Ziba cruelly.

"I can't go with you watching!" I blasted back at him.

They both cracked up and turned their heads.

"We're not watching," Ziba mocked.

With crippled legs, bent and contorted, I squatted, feeling like a dog doing its business on the front lawn. Humiliated, I knew it was a disgusting scene, but it reflected exactly how I felt—how Mephibosheth felt about himself.

15

Later that night, Ziba held out a torn piece of pita-looking bread and some dried fruit for me to take. "You'd better be glad I packed your bag at Machir's house before I came searching for you in the wilderness," he said, rubbing his hand across his mouth. "You'd be dead for sure."

"Thanks," I said with an attitude. "My hero."

"You know what's crazy about all this?" Ziba said, leaning against the chariot.

"No, but I'm sure you're going to tell me." I was on a roll. I didn't like him and he didn't like me.

"You've turned into such a cynic," he quipped, popping a nut in his mouth. "I remember when you were a toddler living in the palace, playing, being ogled over by your parents and grandparents. You could do no wrong. But I was a teenager being groomed to be a servant in Saul's house for the rest of my life. I would look at you and burn with envy. *'Kid's royalty and doesn't even know it. One day he's going to rule. Why couldn't I have been born to royalty?'* While you were living in lavishness, my life was work, work, work." Ziba's eyes became red with rage. His voice grew nasal and irritating. "I got lashed because of you! You see these scars?" he spat, lifting his tunic revealing a series of raised marks like stripes, running across his lower back. "All because of you, you little brat."

"How could I possibly be the blame for that?" I snapped back. "Tell me!"

"I'll tell you how!" he snorted. "Your grandfather Saul was mental. No. He was a raving lunatic! Always obsessing over things—'Don't touch my spear!' 'Don't touch my sword!' 'Don't touch me!' Then he would have conversations with no one like he was hearing voices. All the servants could tell when Saul was having one of his crazy days."

"I've had a couple of those myself," I mumbled under my breath, remembering back as far as my memory would allow.

"Are you paying attention to me? It's like you're in another world."

"I'm listening," I said, rolling my eyes. "You may continue."

"Thanks for your permission," said Ziba sarcastically. "Like I was saying, your grandfather was possessed or something. When he got in one of those moods we tried to hide. Fortunately he brought David in to sing and play the harp. That seemed to calm him down . . . most days. I remember the time it didn't work and he threw his spear at David! I tell you, King Saul was nuts! I think he was jealous of David."

"So I've heard," I said.

"And let me tell you something else. Innocent people got hurt because Saul would act irrationally before thinking things through."

"Irrational," I said. "That sounds just like me."

"What are you talking about?"

"Never mind."

"As I was saying, Saul had this cup. It was made of gold and silver, with artwork carved all over it. The man had a zillion cups, but he was obsessed with that particular one. It had belonged to King Agag—a spoil from battle. I think when he looked at it he got a sense of power. And that's the only cup he'd drink from—always had it by his side like it was his precious kid or something. How weird is that?"

"I remember that cup," I said, as Mephibosheth.

"You should!" snapped Ziba. "I wish I could forget it!"

I blinked and looked at him quizzically. Ziba was as crazy as Saul.

"One day, when you were four or five," he continued, "Saul and your father were out of the palace. I was instructed to clean the outer rooms and the court. Leeba and the women were there watching over you. They thought you were so cute, putting on a show for everyone, making them clap and laugh at everything you did. Then, the shofar blew in the market—a celebration song. Everybody ran out of the palace to see what the commotion was all about. Leeba picked you up and you pitched a royal fit, threw yourself on the ground in a tantrum. 'I'll watch him,' I said like an idiot. 'You go.'

"I figured it would give me a break from all the cleaning. We ran all over the palace, wrestling, playing chase. Before your legs were broken, you were a fast little thing. We were having fun when all of a sudden, something came over you. I remember you glanced at the throne room door and then back at me.

"I sensed what you were scheming and yelled for you to stop. Ignoring my command, you ran into the throne room. How many times had you been told never to go in there?" Ziba glared at me. "How many?"

I tilted my head and shrugged my shoulders, not remembering, but realizing it was pretty important to him.

"I yelled for you to stop, but you looked at me defiantly and darted inside. And you headed straight for the golden cup. The sun was shining through the window, glistening off it. Before I could stop you, you picked up the king's cup and threw it across the room! I couldn't believe it. The cup hit the wall and bounced across the floor. When it came to a stop, it was covered with dents and scratches. When you saw my rage, you shot out of the throne room into the courtyard crying like an innocent victim, straight into Leeba's arms. They were just coming back. Poking out your lower lip, you pointed at me. Leeba comforted you and lit into me for not watching you properly. I was immediately put back to cleaning and forgot about the cup lying on the throne room floor.

"When Saul found it damaged, he was livid! 'Who did this?' he shouted. 'Who dared enter my throne room and touch my cup?' He was so mad that he threw spears at his guards, nipping one on the heel. 'Find who did this!' he ordered.

"I remember when the king summoned me. 'You dared to enter the throne room without permission?' Saul asked me. 'You touched my cup?'

"I tried to explain that you had run into the throne room while I was watching you but he wouldn't listen. Crazy with rage, Saul went for his spear. I thought he was going to drive it through my chest, so I ran—but two guards grabbed me and held me down. Saul began beating me with the handle of his spear. He was so big and intimidating, and I was a scrawny twelve-year-old kid. Saul beat me so hard the flesh on my back was shredded. When I was about to pass out, your father, Jonathan, came into the room.

"He pulled Saul off me and brought me to the physician. When Jonathan found out what really happened, he showed me mercy and kindness. If not for him, Saul would have killed me. From then on Jonathan kept a watchful eye on me. That's how I became King David's servant."

Ziba's eyes narrowed. "But the scars remain—because of you!"

"I'm sorry that happened," I said, as Mephibosheth. "But I was only five. I can't even remember it."

"Life has a way of playing cruel jokes, doesn't it? Now look at us. I live in the palace and you hang out in caves. I have land, crops, and my own servants, and you're not even fit to be my servant!"

"I never read that in the—" I stopped myself. "Bitterness is taking you over, Ziba," I continued. "You're more crippled than Mephibosheth, I mean me."

"You're acting strange," he said. "You've been in the desert too long. The heat's getting to you. I don't know why King David is wasting his time or mine on fetching you."

A passionate fury rose up inside me. I couldn't take his constant degrading of Mephibosheth any longer. "Really, Ziba!" I exclaimed. This was me talking, Nick Gregory. "You act so high and mighty, but you do realize you are still *only* a servant? You'll always be a servant. *Everybody* knows that too! It's written in the—"

"You're a liar—a filthy, jealous liar!" Ziba slapped me with the back of his hand, knocking me against the inside of the chariot bed. Looking at me with disdain, he shook his finger in my face. "At least I'm not a worthless cripple, a dead dog like you! Trust me, you'll get what you deserve, what's coming to you!"

I wiped my busted lip. It stung and was bleeding again.

"You know it's not my fault that I'm crippled," I said pulling myself back into the sitting position. "Leeba dropped me from the wall while escaping the Philistine invasion. She saved my life. I was in line for the throne and she knew the Philistines would kill me. That's why they hid me."

"Leeba should have left you to be executed with the other

royalty," Ziba said, spitting on the ground next to me. "You know what else? Before the fall, your name was Merib-Baal. It meant 'contender with the false god Baal.' Just think. They had big plans for you. You were going to be a mighty warrior or even a king." Ziba reared back his head and let out that irritating laugh again. "But then everything changed. When they hid you in Lo-debar they changed your name to Mephibosheth . . . 'son of shame.' Instead of executing you, God let you live in shame and misery for all these years to punish you."

"You're sick," I said, forcing myself to look into his eyes.

Ziba turned away, apparently emotionally spent from releasing all the pent-up rage. "You'd better get some sleep," he said. "You're going before the king tomorrow. Pray that you find favor in his eyes. But I wouldn't count on it."

The temperature in the desert dropped significantly at night. Ziba and Gaius slept in their bedrolls by the fire. I shivered underneath the coarse blanket in the back of the chariot, gazing at the stars. Never before had I experienced such overwhelming grandeur. No artificial light in competition with them, the stars dazzled—billions of them, flung across the sky like diamond grains of sand by the hand of God. I could feel his creative majesty wrapping around me. Ironic that in this bizarre, messed-up situation, there was still beauty to behold if you just looked for it.

With each minute that passed through the night, the memory of Nick Gregory faded a little bit more. Like most dreams, even the extremely vivid ones, the more time passes, the more details become fuzzy. By the time drowsiness had overtaken me, all I remembered was that I had a daughter, a son, and a wife. Their names had escaped me. Only the feelings of guilt and shame remained.

When I woke the next morning, the memory of Nick Gregory was gone too.

16

Gaius pulled the reins, stopping the chariot on a level spot overlooking the valley. It was still morning and the sun was at our backs peeking over the mountains. I had awakened at dawn when we crossed the Jabbok River and then dozed back off for a couple of hours as we traveled through the rugged terrain known as Gad. It's amazing how much territory two horsepower can cover in that short amount of time.

"Beautiful Jezreel," Gaius yawned, stretching out his arms. Woozy, with a pounding headache, I poked my head up from underneath the blanket. Once I got the gunk out of my eyes and could see clearly, I looked out. A brisk, refreshing morning breeze blew across my face as I gazed at the immense valley stretching before us. Unlike the barren wasteland from which we'd just come, for miles and miles in all directions, as far as the eye could see, was the richest, greenest, most fertile farmland I'd ever seen.

Another river, larger than the Jabbok, snaked its way through the middle of the valley. In the far distance, on the horizon, the river emptied into a bright blue sea that was nestled between two mountain ranges.

"If we keep a steady pace," said Gaius, "we can make it by sundown tomorrow."

"Jerusalem?" I asked.

Ziba looked at me like I'd lost it. "Where do you think we're going, crooked man? Of course, Jerusalem."

Crooked man? I thought. That was a new one. *Didn't take you long to start with the insults, Ziba.*

Ignoring his verbal abuse, I shrugged my shoulders, not seeing a city anywhere, only small villages and farms patched across the valley landscape like a quilt.

"Have you been away so long that you don't even recognize Canaan, the land of milk and honey . . . home?"

"It's more wonderful than they said," I replied, straining my eyes trying to spot a glimpse of Jerusalem but seeing nothing. "Where's the City of David?"

Gaius pointed out over the valley. "You can't see it now," he said. "It looks like a pile of rocks, but it's right on that ridge of mountains across the valley where the Jordan runs into the Salt Sea—the ridge in the middle."

"Let's get going," announced Ziba. "I miss my Alya."

"Your wife?" I asked. I don't know why I even bothered talking to him.

"Yes," said Ziba. His countenance seemed to soften. "And I miss my boys."

It still amazed me that someone had actually married him, that he had sons. Maybe it was one of those arranged marriages. Yeah, that had to be it. Gaius popped the reins. "Get!" There was a jolt and I braced myself.

It took us most of the day to descend the mountain and move deep into the valley. Exhausted, we stopped and ate fresh figs from the trees. Barley swayed in the breeze. Olive trees and pomegranates were hearty and bountiful along with herds of sheep and cattle. Looking around, I had a sense that I'd stood in that very place many years before.

"Don't you miss all this, Mephibosheth?" asked Ziba.

I nodded, my body tired and achy from being banged around in the back of the chariot for so long. An ox-drawn cart loaded with vegetables approached us on the road. One of us was gonna have to give.

"Move aside!" Ziba shouted. "We're on a mission for the king!"

The oxcart moved to the side of the road and stopped. Gaius nodded and gave a slight wave of thanks to the driver as we passed. Ziba haughtily stared straight ahead. The farmer stared at me.

"The land . . . the planting . . . the harvest," said Ziba,

waving his arm over the countryside. "All this was your grand-father's and your father's. It should have been yours."

"Thanks for reminding me," I said, thinking about the vast difference between this breathtaking place abounding with growth and Lo-debar, where nothing grows. It was difficult to grasp that this land had once belonged to my family, that I could have become king.

"I have my own land now, you know, and servants too—about twenty of them," Ziba continued to brag. "Who knows, Mephibosheth, maybe the king will spare your life and make you one of *my* servants? Wouldn't that be an act of mercy? But then again, in your condition you can't even serve! What use are you to me?"

That's about how I was feeling. What use was I to any-one? Even if by some miracle this land became mine again, I wouldn't be able to take care of it. Waves of shame began pounding me like waves thrashing a seashore. I was nothing more than dung. No, I was worse than dung. At least dung was useful for something like fertilizer. I couldn't help but think about how my life could have been if my legs weren't bent and broken. Those days put me in a spiral . . . made me wish this "crooked man," as Ziba had called me, was dead. Living in low places for too long tends to do that to a person. Maybe David would do what Ziba couldn't—put me out of my misery. Yet, as much as I talked and thought about death, I was scared of dying.

The more ground we covered through the valley, the bigger

the ridges and mountains in the distance became. By midafternoon, they were starting to take shape. Though I still couldn't make out much detail, the ridge in the middle was taller, flat-surfaced, and on the top were what I assumed were the walls of the City of David just as Gaius had said.

After traveling for almost three days, we finally reached Jerusalem. The sun was beginning to set, turning the city walls pinkish-orange. A chill of anxiety ran though my arms and back. Now finally, after all these years, King David had found me.

Soldiers who could have passed for Gaius's twins were guarding the gates. Ziba was clearly a minister of the king because as our chariot approached, he nodded and we were ushered through the gate.

"Out of the way!" shouted Ziba at the rubberneckers gawking at the repulsive, less-than-human creature in the back of the chariot. As we made our way through the narrow, winding streets of the city, the inhabitants mingled in front of their shops and homes preparing for the evening. Fires burned in the streets and flames flickered in lamps, giving the clay stucco homes a warm glow.

"Do you remember any of this?" asked Ziba.

"Some," I said. Twenty years in hiding does things to your memory.

The chariot stopped in front of the palace walls, its own city inside the city.

"Get him out," ordered Ziba. "It's time to see the king!"

Gaius hoisted me out of the chariot and stood me on my feet. Wobbling and hunched over, wearing my stinky rags, I clutched my crutches nervously. I was used to people gaping at me, but these folks were different. Adorned in lavish, festive attire, they were clearly the upper class of the kingdom. Now I was more afraid than ever of what the king was going to do when he saw me. Why would he call me here after all these years? I hadn't caused any waves.

Thumping my way through the long hallways of the palace, my legs ached under me. They dragged behind me over the marble floors making a scraping sound, echoing through the chambers, causing Ziba's eyes to roll. "Carry him!" he ordered.

With no sensitivity to my pain or embarrassment, Gaius and another guard who was standing nearby hoisted me onto their shoulders and toted me the rest of the way to the chamber where the king's throne was located. Music was wafting from behind two massive wood and gold doors with detailed artwork etched on them—a lion and bear, a headless Goliath with King David propping his foot on the giant's chest holding up the decapitated head in victory. Guards holding spears swung it open and I was carried though, Ziba by our side, his chest stuck out like he'd won the battle at Mount Gilboa.

"Just put me out of my misery," I muttered under my breath as the music came to a halt and all the beautiful people stopped dancing to watch the filthy cripple being carried past them.

"That's Mephibosheth," they whispered and pointed. Visibly repulsed by my appearance, some didn't whisper.

On the other side of the room, which was really more like an auditorium held up by rows of tall, brightly painted pillars, there were large marble steps leading up to the throne where King David sat. Ziba, Gaius, and the other guard holding me stopped and waited for the king's signal. Standing around King David's throne was an entourage of important-looking men who were engaged in a spirited conversation among themselves, no doubt about me. The king silenced them with a wave of his hand then motioned for us to come forward. I was carried the rest of the way up the steps to the foot of the throne and placed on the floor. Gaius and the other guard bowed to the king and backed away. Ziba also bowed and then stepped aside.

"Well done," David said to Ziba.

"Thank you, my king," said Ziba, placing his hands together in front of his chest and nodding.

Without even looking up at the king, I closed my eyes, stretched out my hands, and fell prostrate to the ground. Face to the floor, I barely whispered under my breath, "Dead dog like me . . . Dead dog like me . . ." a part of me hoping against hope for some sort of mercy, another part of me hoping the sword would fall quickly and end my life of pain.

17

"כלב מת אוהב אותי" . . . (*Dead dog like me*) "כלב מת אוהב אותי"
(*Dead dog like me*) . . . The Hebrew words wrestled their way
out of my mouth slurred and disjointed, garbled. "אוהב אותי
כלב מת" (*Dead dog like me*) . . . My head jerked back and forth.
Then, with one final gasp, one last chance at hope, I lunged
forward and screamed, "נא לא להרוג אותי!" (*Please don't kill me!*)

Gripped in terror, my eyes popped open. Something was
stuck in my throat, choking me. Wheezing in air, I wanted to
tear out the obstruction but couldn't. Like my legs, my arms
betrayed me, refusing to cooperate. I jerked them again and
again, but nothing. My whole body was paralyzed! A blurry
figure now leaned over me. In the fog of disorientation, I could
only make out a silhouette.

"אני פשוט כלב מת. לא לפגוע בי!" *(I'm just a dead dog. Have mercy on me!)* I said.

"It's all right," the figure said, holding my shoulders back in an apparent attempt to restrain and calm me. "It's okay now. You can relax." The voice was soothing and tender—female. "Everything is going to be just fine." Hazy lights shone above her head like multiple halos. *An angel?* My heart rate slowed and the tightness in my chest released. I lay there panting and confused in a puddle of sweat.

"אבל אני—" *(But I—)* my voice cracked, weakly.

"Shh," she whispered. "Don't try to speak."

Gazing up at her, even with my vision blurred, I couldn't help but notice her stunning beauty. And the sweetness of her scent, it seemed familiar somehow as it swept over me.

"מי אתה?" *(Who are you?)* I slurred.

She shook her head. "I'm sorry, Nick, but I don't understand what you are saying. You know—"

Before she could finish her statement, two nurses ran into the room. "His monitor alarm went off," one of them announced.

"He's back," said the woman by my side as she stepped aside.

"Good," the nurse said. "Backing off the meds is working then."

"Something's not right," the woman said. "He's speaking a foreign language!"

The two nurses wasted no time. One took my vitals while

the other adjusted the myriad tubes connected to various parts of my body, assuring both my arms were securely strapped down. One was in a complex brace. My torso from the waist up to my chest was wrapped in a bandage. "This is for your own protection, Mr. Gregory," one of the nurses said. The other one, the heavyset one, shined a penlight in my eyes. I didn't even blink. Slowly she pulled the tube out of my throat.

"השם שלי הוא מפיבושת," (*My name is Mephibosheth,*) I said, exhaling.

"Has he ever spoken this language before?" one of the nurses asked the woman.

"Not to my knowledge," she said, pushing her hair away from her worn and weary eyes. "I've known Nick more than half of my life and he's never spoken a foreign language."

"Strange things happen to the brains of people in comas," the nurse said as she checked the tightness on the cables attached to one of my legs. I was elevated in a type of metal brace. Cables were attached to the brace and the brace was connected to bolts coming out of my leg. *Okay, that can't be good.* My other leg was not elevated but it was in a castlike splint. "I've heard all sorts of stories," the nurse continued. "We had a sixteen-year-old girl once who was in a coma for five days. When she came out she was speaking fluent Chinese! Girl was as Caucasian and American as Abe Lincoln."

"Will this be permanent?" asked the woman.

"Hopefully not," said the nurse. "As Mr. Gregory's system heals, the cognitive memory adjusts in the brain first. Memory of people and events usually develops a little slower. Sometimes a lot slower. The new medication will calm him and hopefully speed up the memory process, but only time will tell. When Dr. Toler checks him, he can tell you more. You just keep on praying like you have been."

"I will," said the woman. "Thanks."

"כאב!" (*Pain!*) I cried out.

18

"Somebody please tell me where I am," I whispered weakly, my words slurred. Another forty-eight hours had passed since they'd brought me out of the medically induced coma. During that time, I'd rouse for short periods then doze back off. The morphine drip kept me pretty drowsy. Each time I woke, a little more of the fog seemed to lift though I was still unaware of who I was, what had happened, or the extent of my condition.

Out of the corner of my eye I could see that the woman who had stood over me when I first came out of it was still in the room, but now curled up sleeping in the reclining chair. Other times when I woke up, she had been by my side patting my hand or touching my arm, never saying much, just things like, "Don't worry. You're going to be fine now" or "Are you in any pain?" Mostly, she looked down at me in pity. Watching her lie there sleeping, I noticed that her clothes had changed, which made me wonder how much time had passed since I'd last dozed off. It was surprising to me that I even remembered such a detail when so many other things were fuzzy.

More alert now and with clearer vision, I could see she had a book with a brown leather cover open on the floor by her chair along with some other books and a big black purse. Instead of trying to speak again, I just continued to watch her sleep, transfixed by her beauty. *Who is she?* I wondered. For some reason, I felt drawn to her as if I knew her, as if she were familiar and we were somehow connected. She twisted in the chair trying to get comfortable, tugging at her sweater. The blanket that was supposed to be covering her had fallen down, and she curled her arms and knees to her chest as if she were cold. I wanted to get up and pull the blanket back over her but I was trapped in the bed, unable to move, my hands strapped down and legs in traction. I could understand my legs not moving since they were clearly damaged, but why were my hands strapped down? I wanted to be free to move, even if it was only in bed. "Argh," I moaned, pulling my wrists up in an attempt to break them loose. But they wouldn't budge, the straps too secure. "Argh!" I growled again, giving one more good tug without any luck. Frustrated, I gave up and let my arms fall limp. When I did, the woman in the chair stirred. Her eyes blinked open, meeting mine.

I tried to speak, but my mouth and brain didn't want to cooperate. She never moved her head, never responded to my slur, just quietly gazed at me with those radiant eyes that drew me in. For the longest time we lay still watching each other, neither speaking. How did I know this woman? Why was she here? Our focus was broken when a nurse came into the room and started taking my vitals. Her stethoscope was on my chest and she was looking at her watch when I slurred, "Where am I?"

"Say it again," said the nurse. There was a small gold cross on her lapel that caught my attention.

"Where am I?" I repeated.

"Stacy, he's speaking English!" said the woman in the chair.

"That's good news," replied Stacy. She looked at me. "You're in the hospital, Mr. Gregory. ICU. It's a miracle you're even alive."

My confusion must have been evident by my expression because the nurse responded with, "Don't try to think too much right now," as she wrapped the blood pressure cuff around my arm. "Your memory is going to be spotty for a while."

I started to speak but she held her finger up for me to be still and then started pumping. After releasing the air pressure she looked up and said with a warm smile, "Okay, now you can talk."

"What's happening?" I asked.

Nurse Stacy looked at the woman sitting in the chair. "Would you like to tell him?"

She nodded and moved to the bedside, took my hand, and squeezed.

"Nick," she said, "You—"

"You're beautiful," I interrupted. "Do I know you?"

"You don't know who I am, Nick?"

"Who's Nick?"

"That's your name," she said. "Your name is Nick."

"No, my name is Mephibosheth."

"Phiba-what?" She squeezed my hand tighter and spoke louder. "You're not making any sense. Your name is Nick Gregory, and I am . . ." She paused long and hard as if she were struggling to find resolve. "I am your wife . . . My name is Abbi."

"Abbi. That's beautiful. But I don—"

She cut me off like I had done her. "You've been in a coma for nearly a month! You were in a terrible car crash."

"No," I slurred, "my name is Mephibosheth. No wife."

Abbi grabbed something out of her purse. "Look, Nick, here's a picture of us," she said holding it up to my face. It was a snapshot of me with my arm around Abbi. She was holding Deuce.

"How did those people get in that little box?" I asked with a puzzled expression.

"It's a cell phone, Nick."

"A what?"

"You talk on it," said Abbi, holding it up to her ear. "It takes pictures. Here, watch." She turned the phone on herself and clicked, then held it out for me to view. "See, it's me."

"Whoa. That's amazing."

Abbi held up the picture of us again.

"That's not me," I protested. "Where is my beard and long hair?"

"Your name is Nick and you've never had a beard or long hair!" She reached back into her purse, took out a small mirror, and held it up to my face.

My eyes narrowed and brow furrowed as I carefully observed the figure staring back at me, eyes sunken deep into their sockets, dark purple circles around them, cheekbones protruding, short hair that hadn't been combed, and scruffy whiskers.

"Who shaved my beard?" I asked more confused than ever as Abbi pulled the mirror back.

"Nobody did," she said. "You never had a beard. See?" She held up the cell phone snapshot to my face again.

"Who's that?" I asked. The guy in the picture didn't look anything like the guy in the bed.

"That's you," she said, clearly frustrated.

My eyes drifted away from me to the dog Abbi was holding. "That dog is cuter than the mangy mutts back home," I said. "What is its name?"

With tears in her eyes, Abbi replied, "Deuce is his name."

"Please don't cry. I like his name."

"I shouldn't have shown you that one."

"Why not?"

"You really don't know, do you?"

I vaguely remembered a flash of light, being in the desert, and Ziba and King David—me lying prostrate before him, pleading for my life. I lifted my hands as much as the straps would allow. My fingernails were clean and trimmed.

"Not Mephibosheth?" I asked.

Stacy began tending to me again. "Like I said," she told Abbi, "we expect him to regain his memory, but it will come in spurts and we don't know how long it will take him to gain full retention."

I had no idea what all that meant so I just smiled, relieved to be out from under the king's wrath. Admiring Abbi's beauty, I had no problem believing that I'd once fallen in love with her. It was happening all over again.

"Why are you so happy all of a sudden?" asked Nurse Stacy.

"Not Mephibosheth," I said, gazing over at Abbi. "She's beautiful."

"Yes, she is," she said.

Alone in the room again with Abbi, though I couldn't remember the details, I felt a deep connection to her and knew instinctively that she was my wife. Something inside me was drawn to her, yet Abbi didn't seem to reciprocate. She was distant and rarely touched me. When she did, it felt dutiful. This puzzled me. I smiled at her and she returned a painful smile.

"I have to go now," she said, patting my hand.

"Please stay," the words slurred out, my hand and arm trembling with weakness.

"Carlee will be here soon," said Abbi, as if that news should reassure me. "She's staying the night with you. I need a break for a little while."

"Who?"

"Carlee . . . our daughter, Nick. We have a daughter."

My eyes lit up as warmness filled my heart. "We have a daughter?"

"Yes, we do."

"I bet she is beautiful like you," I said, laying my head back on the pillow, gazing up at the ceiling. I wanted it to be true.

"She is beautiful," said Abbi. "You'll see soon enough." She patted my hand again and stood up. "I really have to go now."

"Okay," I said, expecting a kiss or a hug from my lovely wife or at least a peck on the forehead. My smile turned to a frown as she turned to walk out. I got nothing.

They say the brain works in mysterious ways, especially when it comes to memory. As Abbi picked up her purse, she turned to me and smiled one more time before leaving the room. It was the smile she did for photos—a learned, posed smile. I'd seen it thousands of times before during our life to-gether. As she flashed that smile, it triggered something in my brain, sparking a single memory. For a split second a picture flashed across my mind's screen and then *poof!* it was gone—a family portrait.

There were four of us.

"Wait!" my voice wheezed out the words as loud as my strength would allow. "We have a son too? He's a baby."

Abbi stopped in midstride halfway through the door. She

turned around, gazing back at me with a look of genuine surprise that morphed into deep sadness. Her forehead wrinkled and the ends of her mouth turned down. Tears forming in her eyes, she stood there in awkward silence, apparently not knowing how to respond.

Perplexed by her reaction, I slurred out the words as best I could. "When I get out of here we are going to Baskin-Robbins—all four of us."

The muscles in Abbi's face began to quiver.

"What's wrong?" I asked.

"Nothing," she said, straightening herself. "I'm fine."

I could tell she was lying.

Maybe it was part pain medicine and part being comatose for a month, but I began to cry uncontrollably, sobbing like a baby. There was no recollection of my wretched past. This time I cried tears of joy because I had such a wonderful family. Abbi cried, too, but I didn't think hers were tears of joy.

Stirred by the commotion, Nurse Stacy came rushing into the room.

"His memory is coming back. He is remembering over twenty years ago!" Abbi said, dabbing her eyes with a tissue. "And he just suddenly burst out crying."

"That's not unusual," said Stacy. "Comatose patients commonly get emotional as things come back to them. It can be quite overwhelming for them."

19

After Abbi left, the pain amped up so I was given more morphine, which put me down for the count. Fourteen hours later, when my eyes blinked open, I felt like I had been run over by a chariot. Groggy and disoriented, every inch of my body seemed to throb. I attempted to lift my hands and arms but couldn't. As the drug-induced haze lifted, I realized I was restricted by the straps. I yanked them a couple of times with my wrists and then gave up, letting them drop. Then I remembered every time I woke up I'd repeat the same routine. How frustrating.

Someone coughed. Turning my head, I saw a woman sitting in the hospital chair across the room. She was not smiling, but appeared troubled. She was also a young woman, wearing a red sweater, jeans, tall suede boots, and a necklace with a cross—the same cross one of the nurses wore. Strange, I could remember things like that, but nothing personal like who I was or why I was in this hospital or who this lovely person was next to me. She seemed familiar and looked like the woman from before, only different. I was confused.

Noticing my moving around, she stood and walked to the edge of my bed and looked down at me. Her eyes were radiant emerald green just like . . .

I looked up at her and smiled. "Wife?"

"No, I'm not your wife," she snapped. "I'm Carlee, your daughter, remember?"

My forehead wrinkled. "No, my daughter is three," I said.

"No, she's not," replied Carlee, pushing her shoulder-length sandy blonde hair behind her ears, clearly unhappy. "She's nearly twenty-three, and I'm her."

I strained my mind grasping for something, some memory of her. "I'm trying to remember," I said, "but I can't. I'm sorry."

"Well, that kind of stuff happens to people who drive themselves into concrete poles!" she said, backing away from the bed, arms crossed over her chest.

"What?" I said. "Why would you say something like that? That's mean."

"Look, Daddy," she huffed, "what you did hurt a lot of people. It was cruel and selfish."

"I don't know what you're talking about. Why are you doing this?" I said, starting to panic. My breaths became short and my heart rate elevated. Panting, my heart monitor went off and nurses burst into the room. Carlee stepped back as they checked my vitals and gave me some more meds to calm me.

Turning to Carlee, the nurse asked, "What happened?" It was the one with the cross, Nurse Stacy.

Carlee's expression shifted to a more worried look. She seemed conflicted. "I upset him," she said. "Maybe it would be better if I just left." She turned and started walking out.

"Wait!" I said, beginning to relax. "Nurse, is it true she's my daughter?"

Carlee stopped halfway to the door. When she turned around tears were in her eyes. The nurse looked at Carlee and then me. "Yes, she is." Turning back to Carlee she continued, "Look, I can't have you upsetting him like that. He needs to rest so his body can mend. Do you understand?"

"Yes, I understand," said Carlee. "I'm leaving anyhow." Turning to me she said, "Daddy, I know you don't remember so you can't understand what I'm feeling. But trust me, for my own sake and yours, I have to go."

"But there's so much I don't know . . . about you . . . about myself."

"Please, I have to go."

"Where's your brother?" I blurted out in desperation. "Can I see him? If you're almost twenty-three, he must be around nineteen, right?"

Carlee couldn't hide the shock on her face. After a moment she said, "Let it go, Daddy. Your memory will come back soon enough and you may wish it hadn't."

"But—"

"It's okay. I still love you even if you do make me crazy," she said and walked out the door.

The pain that shot through my heart was much worse than the pain in my crushed and shattered body.

The rest of the morning I tossed and turned in the bed, trying to force memories into my head, getting nothing but a migraine. I could only fuzzily remember the photo that had momentarily flashed through my mind of the four of us twenty years earlier. *Who am I? What have I done? My son? Why won't Carlee tell me about him? Why are she and my wife so distant and upset with me? Did I really drive myself into a concrete pole?*

The nurse, yes, the nurse! I realized. *Maybe she knows something about me.* I pushed the Call Nurse button, and a few minutes later a young nurse I had not seen before entered my room. Her scrubs were blue, not white like the others'. Her long hair was black and straight, pulled back into a ponytail. Younger-looking than Carlee, the name on her tag said "Rachel."

"What can I help you with?" Rachel said, bright and cheery.

"Where's Stacy?" I asked.

"She left for the day, so you got me." She beamed.

"How old are you?"

"Twenty-one," she said enthusiastically. "I just graduated nursing school."

"Congratulations."

"Thank you!"

"My daughter is twenty-two," I said. "She just left."

"I know. I've met her," said Rachel. "Very pretty! You must be proud."

"Yes, very."

"You pushed your button, Mr. Gregory," she said, looking eager to serve. "What do you need?"

Looking at her I thought, *Surely she doesn't know anything about my personal life. There are hundreds of patients in this hospital and she's so young.*

"Can we just talk for a minute?"

"Sure, Mr. Gregory. What do you want to talk about?"

"Who am I, Rachel?" I asked. "Do you know anything about me?"

Her face lit up. "Why, everybody knows who you are," she said, ponytail bobbing. "You're the famous Nick Gregory!"

"Famous?"

"Yes sir," she said. "You write books and preach on TV. I can't believe I'm actually your nurse. I've never served anyone famous before!"

"Preach?"

"Yes sir. You were the pastor of a very big church."

"Were?"

"Yes sir."

That didn't really make sense to me, so I just kept going. "My son," I said. "Do you know anything about him?"

Initially Rachel seemed taken back by the question, but then she turned sympathetic. She took my hand and squeezed. "No one told you?"

I shook my head.

"Your son died, Mr. Gregory," she said compassionately. "Like, a year ago. It was all over the news. I'm so sorry."

I dropped my head back onto the pillow. "My son," I whispered. "You can go now."

I don't know how long I lay there thinking about Rachel's words—*"Your son died, Mr. Gregory . . . Your son died, Mr. Gregory . . ."* The more I pushed my memory banks, the more rage pumped through me. Then I snapped, just like I had in the front yard that day, exploding, trying to rip my arms loose from their constraints, jerking my hands around like a crazy person, but of course they wouldn't budge. I pulled and yanked and twisted until there were burns on my wrists. I thrashed violently enough to dislodge some of the monitoring devices. I was now in severe pain but my adrenaline kept me moving.

"I have to get out of here!" I screamed. "Let me out!" All sorts of beeps and alarms went off, and nurses rushed into the room, including Rachel. Realizing she'd messed up by telling me what she did, Rachel started to cry. Me, you would have thought I was cried out, that there wouldn't be single tear left. Yet, when I saw Rachel cry, I broke down and began to sob too. I knew no details. No reasons. I only wept for my son, the son I would never see again. The flood of meds washed over me relaxing my body. I needed to be calm because something else would happen that night. The grief over Philip's death triggered my brain, and the memories came flooding back—all of them, a lifetime crammed into one single night. I felt like

I was in a science fiction movie, strapped down with a mad scientist downloading information into my brain. Memories were coming hard and fast. And when they came, they came with a vengeance.

Now I understood why Abbi was so distant. I couldn't believe she had even stayed at the hospital with me. Carlee—my sweet daughter, how I'd let her down. I checked out rather than stepping up and coming through for her. Deuce—I ran over my companion, my buddy, my friend. And my son, Philip—how could I have let things get to that point? I was a complete failure in the things that really mattered.

Pictures flashing through my mind of those I loved and had now lost, it was a dark night. Gone were the sentimental feelings about my family and imaginings of a happy reunion after all this hospital time. Those possibilities were now replaced with anger and bitterness, bitterness at God and myself—mostly myself. How could I have taken my wonderful wife and family for granted? Things seemed so clear now. There was no good in me. Nothing. Despair overwhelmed me. "God," I said under my breath. "Help me! Forgive me. I need to know you are here! Why didn't you let me die?" No sooner had the words slipped out of my mouth than a nurse came into the room. It was Stacy.

I must have looked pretty pathetic. She patted my arm sympathetically and smiled. "It's morning, Mr. Gregory. Time to take those vitals." She dove right in. "Heard you had a really rough night."

"The roughest yet."

Unwinding her stethoscope from her neck, she said, "Can I get you anything?"

"Can you please find a Bible and read to me?"

Seeming surprised at the request, she stammered, "There's a Gideon Bible right here in this drawer." She took the brown hardback Bible out of the drawer. "What do you want me to read?"

"I'm losing it here, Stacy. Can you please just read me something? I see that cross on your lapel. Read something, anything I can grab hold of!"

Stacy paused for a moment, thinking. Then she began flipping through the pages until she found what she was searching for. "Here in Second Corinthians, listen to this. I heard it this morning on the radio. I think it fits the situation. *'We were under great pressure, far beyond our ability to endure, so that we despaired of life itself. Indeed, we felt we had received the sentence of death. But this happened that we might not rely on ourselves but on God, who raises the dead.'*"

Stacy lowered the Bible, an intent look about her. "Now you would think that it would be all the great and wonderful things in life that would lead us to depend on God," she said. "But that's not what I just read. It says Paul despaired. Paul had moments of depression and anxiety. Then it says he was burdened beyond his ability to endure. In other words, what Paul was going through was bigger than his ability to fix it. It was those ugly, hard things in his life that taught him to depend on God, who raises the dead. Just think, Mr. Gregory, even the great apostle Paul fell into despair. I don't know about you, but that gives me some hope."

"Thank you, Stacy. That helps."

20

"I'm gonna be honest with you," Dr. Toler began, his voice stern, eyes locked on to mine. Late sixties, tall, lanky, with silver hair, his white coat hanging over a slightly hunched body, I could tell right off that he was old school. He seemed like a straight shooter—the sooner they know the truth, the sooner they can deal with it.

Abbi wasn't there. Dr. Toler had informed her that I'd regained most of my memory and of my violent outburst. She obviously chose to stay away for a while. The doctor thought it was for the best, saying I could use some time to process everything, that after he explained to me the extent of my injuries they would bring in a psychiatrist to assess my emotional status. In other words, to determine if I was a box of crazy flakes and still a threat to myself. *Great, can't wait for that one.*

"You don't think I tried to kill myself, do you? Clearly it was a terrible accident."

He lowered his glasses. As he gazed at me I could tell he knew the truth. "We have to cover our bases," he said.

Because I was in ICU, visitation had been strictly limited to immediate family and those approved by Abbi. Presently, that amounted to no one, and without anyone there, the next twenty-four hours were lonely and torturous. I remembered Abbi had served the divorce papers to me, but I still longed to see her. I was allowed to use my cell phone, but only if someone was in the room watching me because they had to unstrap my arms. I texted Abbi three times with no response. My eighty-four-year-old mother called. Thank the Lord for moms! She loved me no matter what stupid, crazy, messed-up excuse for a son I was. It was comforting. My two brothers and sister also called, which was unexpected yet appreciated. My extended family didn't have much interaction, except on holidays. They all lived in Topeka, Kansas—twelve hundred miles from me. Everyone was busy with their own families. Maria called, bless her. So many people from Grace Life Church and ministries around the world called that I couldn't possibly answer them. They left messages but before long my voice mail box was full. Evidently they'd been getting reports on my progress.

"I don't know much about God," Dr. Toler continued. "But I believe you tried to kill yourself, which seems pretty odd for a preacher. We'll let that be our little secret for now. All I can say is if God is up there, he must have been looking out for you. People who witnessed the crash said it was horrific. Your SUV looked like a bomb had detonated inside it—was all over the news. The engine relocated to the trunk. You went right through the windshield. I don't throw the word *miracle* around very often. I can't even recall the last time I used it. But it's a miracle you're still here. Do you know how much blood you lost?"

I shook my head.

"A whole lot. Two of your major arteries were completely severed." He pulled off his glasses, cleaned them with a cloth from his coat pocket, and placed them back on before he continued. "Much better," he said. "Thirteen broken bones. A collapsed lung. Your intestines were mush. You were in such bad shape, the paramedics wanted to take you straight to the morgue. They were sure you wouldn't make it to the hospital. One of the paramedics insisted that since you had a flicker of a heartbeat they needed to give ER a sporting chance. You need to find that guy and kiss his feet. The ER doctors didn't give you a shot of making it. At first, they didn't even want to open you up. If I were you, I'd be trying to find out why the Good Lord saw fit to keep you here on this earth. I suspect you saw angels or something when you were out, come back with a message to the world, and are gonna write a book about it."

"I hate to disappoint you, Doc," I said cynically. "I didn't see the great white light or any angels. My aunt Susie wasn't there to meet me either. Only some crippled guy." I looked down at my body in traction. "What about all this?"

"Yeah, about that," Dr. Toler said. "It's interesting that you mentioned a crippled guy."

I braced myself for his next words.

"Your legs and hips were crushed—femur, tibia, lateral halves of the innominate pelvic. Your thoracic and lumbar bones were shattered."

"Speak English, Doc."

"Your back was broken. We've had to basically rebuild you. You know, pins, plates, screws, and rods. You name it. You got it. The good news is somehow your spinal cord is fine. You're not paralyzed. But we had to keep you strapped down to ensure you didn't damage your spine. It was badly bruised. So we couldn't take any chances."

"I thought that was to keep me from . . . you know . . ."

"Trying to kill yourself again?"

"Yeah," I said sheepishly.

"That too," he said.

He looked down for a moment and scribbled something on his clipboard. Then he leaned forward, clenched his fist, and fixed his eyes intently on mine. "The bad news is you will never walk normally again," he said. "You've had two surgeries. Even with extensive therapy you'll still be seriously handicapped. I hesitate to use that word. You will walk with a severe limp, surely with some sort of aid. If rehab goes well, in a year you might get by with only a cane."

A memory of Mephibosheth flashed through my mind—him hobbling around in the dirt, sitting at the nearly dried-up well in Lo-debar, begging for alms. I don't know where the memory came from, because I had not experienced that one.

"You're going to need several more surgeries beginning once you gain your weight back," the doctor said. Because of my intestinal issues and having a feeding tube, I was down to a mere 155 pounds, sixty pounds lighter than my normal weight of 215.

Now at that moment you would have thought I would've exploded or cried or tried to rip my arms out of the restraints or something. Instead, I simply looked at him and said, "That figures. I deserve it."

"Nobody deserves this," said Dr. Toler. He patted me on the shoulder and walked out.

21

For the next week Dr. Fry, the shrink, came in once in the morning and once in the evening to do his assessment. He seemed nice enough and really wanted to help me. The problem was, I didn't want his help. From the onset, I gave him a difficult time, which probably put him on the defensive. I have to say, though, he was a good listener and very patient. When I was condescending in my tone, which was often, he would simply nod.

With every tick of the round clock on the wall and every memory that came back, I was becoming more and more depressed. I desperately wanted to see Abbi and Carlee, but I understood why they were staying away. Who could blame them? The dark cloud swallowed me again. The voice was back, taunting. "*Nikky boy, you're a worthless piece of stinky flesh lying in that bed. You're just like old Mephibosheth. You're a dead dog!*"

Dr. Fry knew I was struggling.

"Let's revisit the events leading up to the crash," he said, his legs crossed, pen in the corner of his mouth, leaning toward me trying to give me his full concentration. "Tell me how you were feeling. Talk to me."

"What's to talk about?" I said. "I'm a dead dog, just like Mephibosheth."

"Like who?" he asked.

"He's a guy in the Bible," I replied. "You wouldn't know anything about that."

"Try me," he said.

"Well, to start with, his life was terrible. He was a pathetic cripple who lived in a barren desert. In ancient Israel being called a dog was an incredible insult."

"I can only imagine," said Fry.

"It's true," I said. "Back then most dogs weren't domesticated pets like they are today, you know. Most were mangy scavengers roaming the cities and countryside feeding off carcasses and rummaging through the dumps. When a dog died, it was left to rot. If someone called you a dog, that was an insult, but being called a 'dead dog' was as bad as you could get. This guy Mephibosheth called himself a 'dead dog'!"

"I see," said Dr. Fry. "And is that how you feel about yourself?"

"Yes sir, it sure is. I feel worse than a dead dog. It pretty much sums up my life right now. You know I wrote a paper on Mephibosheth in seminary. "

"You did?" he said. "That's interesting." Then he suddenly began scribbling some notes on his pad. When finished, he calmly folded his hands and returned his attention to me.

"Okay," I said. "What are you writing, that I'm delusional or something? That I tried to kill myself, ran off my wife and daughter, ran over my dog, and caused my son to OD?"

Dr. Fry looked at me and said, "To quote from your book, 'We're all broken but exceedingly valuable.'"

Just then my cell phone dinged indicating a text message. My face lit up as I picked it up and read. "It's Abbi!" I exclaimed. "She's coming tomorrow!"

22

Abbi stopped in the hallway a few feet shy of the hospital room door, stalling a moment to gather herself. She took a couple of deep breaths and straightened her outfit—a navy skirt that came just above the knees, navy high heels, matching blazer with a cream silk blouse that accented her auburn hair and fair skin. She'd had several meetings that day to take care of some business—a press conference, a financial meeting, and then her attorney. Unzipping her purse, Abbi glanced yet again at the papers inside. Why was she so afraid? She knew what she had to do.

Nick was asleep when Abbi walked into the room, so she scooted the chair next to the bed and sat down watching the man she once loved, reminiscing.

* * *

It had been a long, hard pregnancy. Carlee was determined to come into the world fighting, and Abbi was tired, dog tired. But not Nick. At least if he was, he wasn't showing it. From the moment she made the big announcement, it was like he wore a cape and spandex and had a big S plastered across his chest. He treated Abbi like a queen, cooking, cleaning, rubbing her feet, waiting on her hand and foot. She could feel the love pouring from him, for her and their daughter still in the womb. Even before the baby bump started to show, every night in bed, Nick would lay his hand on Abbi's stomach and pray. The prayers were always the same. "Lord, thank you for the most amazing, wonderful, and beautiful wife! I thank you for her love, friendship, and partnership. But most of all, I thank you that she's a godly woman and is going to be a godly mother. Now I ask you to place your divine favor and blessing on this child in her womb. We commit her to you. And Father, empower me to be the godly husband and father they need me to be. Amen."

The labor was long and intense, but Nick held her hand the whole way, even when Abbi almost twisted it off his body during the final pushes. She dug her nails into his arm, but he never let her see his discomfort. That's the way their marriage had been. She could lean on him and he never flinched, standing strong like the oaks outside their beautiful home.

When Carlee was delivered, the pain subsided and Nick cut

her cord of life. Carlee was wrapped in a blanket, handed to the new mother, and the three of them embraced.

"I'm so proud of you, honey," Nick said, kissing Abbi. "You are a warrior."

At that moment, in addition to the wonderment of giving birth, gazing in awe at the miracle that was their daughter, Nick had made Abbi feel like she was the most incredible wife and mother on the planet. She was so happy.

* * *

"Oh Nick," Abbi sighed. "What happened?" She remembered the sudden and massive growth at the church. Everything had become about the numbers—more, bigger, better. Then the success of the television broadcasts and the books, all the people groveling at Nick's feet. The power. At first it all seemed exciting and innocent enough, but Abbi sometimes sensed uneasiness in her spirit. Every time she confronted Nick about it, he would enthusiastically and charismatically explain to her all the great things God was doing and she would inevitably give in. Nick had an uncanny ability to persuade people. And after all, who could argue with God's blessing? Reaching and helping more people was such a good thing. Souls were being saved. Lives were being changed. They felt like they were moving with God, following the path he laid before them. It was easy to just go with the flow and thank God for his faithfulness and blessings. But not all lives were changed for the better. It was somewhat subtle and deceptive. Behind the scenes there were power struggles. Some of the things that went on were not very godly or Christlike. Some lives were changed, all right. They were crushed and broken, their faith shipwrecked and shattered. Abbi had sat in on a number of confrontations that made her wish she had a house in the country where only her family and close friends knew who they were.

Then she remembered Philip, the suicide note, Nick's betrayal. Anger and bitterness began to rise up inside her all over again. "Help me, Lord," she prayed. Angry with herself, she reached in her purse and pulled out her iPhone and opened her Bible app. Grasping for hope she clicked on Psalms. *"Commit your way to the LORD,"* she read. The Psalms were Abbi's favorite, especially when she was hurting. *"Trust in him and he will do this: he will make your righteous reward shine like the dawn, your vindication like the noonday sun. Be still before the LORD and wait patiently for him . . ."*

"Lord," Abbi whispered, "shine your light on me and show me that I'm doing the right thing."

23

I knew Abbi was coming, but when I awoke the next morning, I didn't expect her to be sitting by my side. I groaned, not from seeing her, but because my legs were aching, which Dr. Toler assured me was a good thing. Being fully out of the coma meant fully feeling the pain, both physical and emotional. He wasn't lying.

"Thanks for coming," I said softly, wincing.

"I'll get the nurse," she said. "She can get you some more pain medicine." Abbi rose to go, but I gripped her hand and held her there, scared she'd leave the room and not come back. The restraints had been removed from my arms. My spine was healing nicely and Dr. Fry had determined that I was not a threat to myself any longer.

"I'm fine," I said. "Please sit back down."

When Abbi sat, I saw it. How had I not noticed it before? I guess I was so focused on her eyes. The memories were clear now, very clear. "That necklace," I said. "I gave it to you for our twentieth anniversary. You're wearing it."

"Yes," said Abbi, clutching the pearls in her hand. "Nick, I came here because we need to talk. Are you up to it?"

I might have been a busted-up fool, but I was not stupid. "Now's as good a time as any," I told her. There was no anger in my voice. I understood perfectly why Abbi was doing this. She married a dead dog who had let her down in so many ways.

Abbi reached into her purse, but before she could pull out what she wanted, a nurse came in to take my vitals and to give me my daily meds. Abbi stood up again and moved out of the nurse's way while he did his thing.

"Stacy and Rachel are out today?" I asked the male nurse.

"Yes sir," he said and started the routine. When finished, he patted my arm and said, "Your vitals are getting stronger, Mr. Gregory. If you need anything, just buzz me."

I could tell Abbi was getting antsy, and as soon as the nurse left, she said, "You know, Nick, this really is not a good time. I shouldn't have come."

"Yes, you should have," I said sharply. "I understand what you have to do. You deserve better than this." I waved my arms across my broken body. "You don't need to be married to a cripple. Let's just get it over with, okay?"

"Do you still not get it, Nick?" she said, with a sharpness in her tone. "Being physically crippled is not where you are handicapped."

Okay, that wasn't what I expected.

Abbi reached inside her purse again and gripped the papers.

"Before I sign those," I said, "I need to tell you that I am truly sorry. I really am. I didn't mean for any of this to happen. I loved Philip! He was our son. And us, Abbi. I can't believe I put the ministry before my family. It was a huge mistake. I just got so caught up. I thought I was doing what God wanted me to do. I was self-righteous and arrogant. And Deuce was an accident. I would never intentionally hurt him. I wouldn't hurt any of you intentionally. You have to know that."

Abbi's face twisted. "Words mean nothing to me anymore," she said.

"What about Deuce?" I asked. "Is he—?"

"Dead?" she said. "Is Deuce dead? Is that what you are trying to say?" Her head and shoulders slumped.

I swallowed hard.

"No, Deuce isn't dead," she said, slowly looking up at me, "but you messed him up pretty bad. Dr. Conroy saved him from the clutches of death. He survived, but—"

"But what?"

Abbi cringed. "His back legs and hips are crushed. He's getting therapy but he'll be severely crippled for life."

I let out a deep and long sigh. "Just like me," I mumbled,

staring up at the ceiling, the memory of how he'd saved my life that morning flashing through my head.

"Yep, Nick, just like you," she said. "I know you didn't mean to run over Deuce, that I can forgive, but Philip . . . how you treated him and what you kept from me . . ." Abbi's face was angry now. I knew the look. It was the look she gave when someone messed with one of her babies. She waved her arm across the bed, pointing to the cables and rods coming from my legs. "You, you did *this* to yourself! And what happened to Philip?" she continued. "What you did to Philip—that was betrayal too!"

She wasn't crying. There was fury in her eyes. A switch had been flipped.

"I don't know what to do, Abbi," I said, my voice cracking.

"What *can* you do, Nick, bring him back?" she spoke loudly, sternly.

"Abbi . . . I . . ."

"Shut up! You make me want to vomit!"

* * *

Abbi's phone had lit up with text messages and voice mails only seconds after her plane hit the tarmac at Dulles International that day. While she was airborne, Nick's sixty-seven-second rampage was going viral. Confused by all the messages, the first thing she did after she got off the plane was to view the YouTube video on her cell phone. Walking through the corridor, she noticed it playing on one of the televisions in a coffee shop as well.

Stunned and in disbelief, Abbi staggered and had to sit. So many emotions were running through her head. First was poor Deuce. Was he even alive? Then, after watching the footage of Nick coming out the animal clinic, she wanted to hide. Finally, she called Nick. There was no answer, so she texted him. After still no reply, she got to her car and drove straight to the animal clinic.

Dr. Conroy was there to meet her in the lobby and whisk her to Deuce, who was just beginning to stir awake from the anesthesia. He perked up when he saw Abbi.

Abbi leaned over Deuce and carefully laid her head on his side. She gently stroked him and kissed the top of his head. "You're a good boy, Deuce," she said, choking back the tears. "I love you." Deuce let out a slight whine of affection. His little ears lifted and then dropped.

"His back legs are crushed," said Dr. Conroy. "He's going to need lots of rehab. There are also internal injuries. He still may not pull through. You never know about these things. I hate to even mention it, but some choose to put their pets down in these circumstances."

"Never!" said Abbi. "Deuce is here for a reason. I know it. He's needed."

Dr. Mary Conroy's boundaries were professional, but she could sense Abbi's pain for more than just Deuce. "I feel your anguish," she said, touching Abbi on the shoulder. "If you need a friend or someone to talk to, I'm here."

Abbi showed a tender smile, her head tilted slightly. "Thank you, Dr. Conroy. I appreciate the gesture. I really do."

On the drive home from the clinic there was still no response from Nick. Something's going on, *she thought, calling and texting him one more time.* I wonder if he got the papers?

With the tinted windows rolled up in her Lexus, Abbi tried her best to ignore the media and protestors lined up in front of the house. Easing up to the gate, it was almost impossible not to read all the hateful signs, so she blasted her Bon Jovi music to drown out the shouting.

Once in the house, Abbi dropped her keys on the kitchen counter and headed toward the bedroom to collapse and regroup. She looked up to find Maria calmly folding laundry in front of the living room television.

"Maria!" Abbi said surprised. "I didn't know you were here." Abbi gave her a quick embrace. "It's good to see you, Maria."

"It's good to see you, too, Señora Abbi."

"Have you seen Nick since what happened?" asked Abbi anxiously.

"Oh, sí," said Maria. "It's been quite a morning."

Maria's calm and compassionate presence caused a sudden release of Abbi's pent-up emotions. She began to shake and dropped down on the sofa. Maria put aside the laundry and sat down beside her.

"Oh Maria," Abbi said. She rested her head on Maria's shoulder and started crying. She cried at the shock of everything that had happened, the grief of it, the pain. She sobbed and sobbed,

Maria holding her and patting her shoulder. After a few minutes, Abbi pulled away. "Just look at me," she said, nose red and puffy, makeup smeared. "I'm a mess." Maria took a tissue out of her apron and handed it to Abbi. Leaning back and dabbing her eyes, Abbi said, "I guess you probably figured out that I filed for divorce."

"Sí, señora."

Abbi sniffed. "Cruel me, right?"

"This is a difficult situation," said Maria. "There are no easy answers, Señora Abbi."

"What am I going to do?"

Maria placed her hands on Abbi's shoulders, her own eyes misty. "I don't want to sound overly spiritual, señora, but please seek the Lord in this. Don't let your anger and bitterness blind you. I know how badly you must be hurting. I know you want out. But give God time to do something. He's working, Señora Abbi. I know the real Señor G. You know the real Señor G too."

"That's just it, Maria. I don't know the real Nick anymore. I thought I did, but he kept too much from me for so long."

"Sí."

"But it hurts so much," said Abbi.

"Sí, sí," said Maria, pulling Abbi into another embrace. They held each other for a long moment.

"I love you, Maria," said Abbi, dabbing her eyes again.

At that precise moment Abbi's cell phone beeped with the word Emergency *attached to the incoming number. "Hello," she reluctantly answered. There was a long pause as Abbi only listened and nodded. Then she gasped, placing her hand over her mouth.*

"That was the police," she said to Maria, her voice coming from somewhere deep inside her throat. "Nick's been in a horrible accident. He may not make it."

As the two women rushed to the hospital so many emotions rushed through Abbi's mind—the whole gamut from guilt, to rage, to fear. Despite all her anger toward him, the thought of Nick dying filled her with deep grief, like a part of her was dying too. Maybe somewhere underneath all the hurt she was feeling, there was something left, a flicker of hope.

* * *

Being in the hospital a month and a half had kept Nick from signing the papers that had been served that day. Now, here she was, standing in front of him in his hospital room, holding them again. With trembling hands Abbi began to silently read.

24

After a few moments scanning, Abbi let the hand holding the papers drop to her side and shifted her focus to me. Eyes narrowing, she tapped the papers against her thigh nervously. Even angry, she was beautiful to me, beautifully intimidating. Abbi clearly held the power now.

"I guess I need to sign those," I said in a pitiful tone. I wasn't to the point of groveling, but I was close. "Let's get this process under way. By the time I'm outta here, it'll all be official and you can move on."

"Just stop!" she said, her voice quick and sharp. "I don't feel a bit sorry for you, Nick, so don't say a word!" Both of Abbi's hands were now planted firmly on her hips, one fist clutching the papers, crunching them. "Before we take another step, you need to understand something!"

"I think I understand, Abbi," I said. "You made it crystal clear on the papers you served."

"No, I don't think you *do*," said Abbi. "You're a selfish coward! Everything is about you. It's always about you! You'll never know how deeply you hurt me—hurt this family, what's left of it. Did Carlee even tell you that she was engaged?"

I lifted an eyebrow. "No, she didn't tell me that."

"Of course she didn't. You want to know why?"

The tongue-lashing had me speechless.

"Because now, after this latest media fiasco involving her father, the great Nick Gregory, her fiancé backed out—told Carlee he couldn't handle it, that the timing wasn't right. She's devastated!"

Closing my eyes, I banged my head back against the pillow, loathing myself. "I don't deserve you guys," I said. "I'm just a dead dog."

"Would you stop it already with the 'dead dog' bit?" Abbi said, a raw edge to her voice. "Why do you keep saying that? Does it have anything to do with Deuce? I told you, he didn't die."

"It has to do with me hating myself right now."

"Hating yourself? Well, how do you like the sound of this?" she continued, glaring at me. "Deuce lived and you're going to live, too, Nick. I'm going to make sure of that! Carlee needs a father who loves her more than he loves himself, and if she ever does get married, her babies are going to need a grandfather!" Abbi glanced down at the papers she was clutching in her hand. "Oh, you're going to live, all right! You're not dying on us after all we've been through." Then suddenly, as if torn herself, she cried out, "God, help me!" and ripped the papers in half, letting the pieces fall to the floor.

My breath stopped and a lump formed in my throat. *Did I just see what I thought I saw?* I lay there stunned, staring at Abbi. *Is the medication causing an illusion?* Yet the torn-up divorce papers were strewn all over the hospital room floor. Abbi was still standing there, foot tapping, arms crossed over her chest. She wasn't crying. She wasn't smiling.

Finally, words stammered out of my mouth. "Wha . . . I . . . I thought . . ."

Abbi paused a moment before responding. "A lot has happened since your crash, Nick. I can't tell you all of it yet," she said. "It's between me and God. But know this, I can't continue with things as they were. I won't. You have to figure this out and I don't mean a year from now. Are you the Nick I pledged to love and honor, or are you that other guy?"

"Wow, okay, so let me see if I'm hearing you correctly," I said. "You're giving me a second chance even though you feel betrayed, you despise me, and you don't know if you can forgive me?"

"God is the One who's giving you a second chance here," said Abbi as she headed for the door. "And he'd better do a miracle."

* * *

"*Abbbbeeegail,*" the voice poked. "*You know you're crazy. What makes you think Nick's going to change? Besides, he's ruined everything. You know you can't trust him. He's sneaky and he's a liar. You're falling right into his trap.*" Abbi tossed and turned in bed, throwing off the covers, sweating though it was only forty degrees outside. "*Come on, Abbi,*" the voice persisted. "*You've thought through this. That's why you went to Florida, remember? Divorce is the right thing, the only way for you to be happy again. Just get the papers signed and get on with it! Have your freedom.*"

Abbi's eyes popped open, her body shaking. "Am I crazy?" she mumbled to herself. "I do deserve to be happy." She peeked out from under the pillow to the digital clock. The glowing green numbers read 2:11. "God," she whispered, "am I doing the right thing? Am I letting him manipulate me?" Curling up in a fetal position, she closed her eyes again and tried to will herself to sleep, but it wasn't happening.

"*Abbeeegail . . . You're not listening. If you stay with Nick you're going to be miserable. And you know God doesn't want you to be miserable. After everything you've done, you should be happy. And look at the mess he's put you in. His messes are your messes as long as you stay with him, Abbi. He's ruining everything you worked so hard for. That's what you get for doing all the right things.*"

Forcing herself out of the bed, she threw on a robe and slippers and began pacing anxiously through the house. In the kitchen, she peeked at Deuce, who was conked out on his special pallet. "Thank you, Lord, for Deuce's recovery," she said. Abbi wanted to check his wounds and bandages and adjust his braces like Dr. Conroy had instructed. But the nightly medicine kept him sleeping soundly, so she would have to wait and tend him in the morning before taking him in for treatment.

Abbi paused at the patio doors leading out to the pool. *So many happy times out there.* She threw on a jacket hanging by the door and stepped outside. The chilly night air was refreshing. Circling the pool she noticed a dark spot at the bottom. Looking more closely, she saw it was her pistol. *What in the world is my pistol doing in the pool? Crazy.*

Inside, Abbi walked on down the hall, past the hole in the wall that Nick had punched, and continued on to his office. Stepping through the door, her foot landed on a piece of broken crystal. Thankful she was wearing her slippers, she noticed the shattered eagle on the floor along with the torn Bible and strewn pages. *Why is this place not cleaned up?* Then she remembered Maria had told her that Nick gave strict instructions *not* to clean it. *So the gun is at the bottom of the pool and the office is trashed. This is not like Nick.* Something more was going on. Abbi stood still for a moment, taking in the scene around her. Then slowly she bent over, picked up the Bible, and began reading the inscription she had written years earlier.

Congratulations, Nick! You've studied so hard and God is going to reward your faithfulness to his call. I'm honored to be your partner in life and ministry. We're a team—

"Abbeeegail, there's no 'I' in team."

She dropped the Bible back on the floor.

"You know it's true. Ha, ha, ha."

"All right," Abbi ordered. "I've had enough of you! In the name of Jesus, I command you to leave this house now!" As soon as the words came out of her mouth, the evil presence lifted and a peace filled the room. At that moment, Abbi had a flash of clarity regarding Nick. He was being tormented by those very same spirits—the voices in her head. His irrational behavior was being driven by the enemy. Nick needed her support, her prayers.

Abbi refocused, scanning her husband's office. Looking for what she came in there for, Abbi couldn't help noticing all the books. Over the years, Nick's library had expanded, even with his new e-reader. Abbi could never miss with a gift of a book at Christmas or his birthday.

In addition to paintings and photos, the walls were adorned with framed covers of the books Nick had authored along with countless articles he'd written and awards received. Once, she had been proud. Now all of it turned her stomach. "Jesus didn't get any awards," she mumbled. Abbi wasn't against writing books. She loved reading as much as anyone. It was just that writing books had become Nick's obsession, his idol. He couldn't lay it down. She knew he'd been called to write and to preach, but something, somewhere had gone askew.

"Oh, come on. I know it's in here somewhere. Where is it?" Abbi knew what she was looking for. For years it had been hanging in the corner above the end table and lamp. Like the books, they had tons of pictures—in albums, on their phones and computers, hanging around the house. But this particular picture was special. It had been Nick's first memory after he came out of the coma. It was also their first family portrait with Philip. Abbi remembered the day as clearly as if it had been yesterday.

* * *

Philip was only six months old and Carlee was three and a half. The four of them got all dressed up and piled in the old Buick LeSabre Nick's dad had given them. Nick called it "The Tank." They headed to the Olan Mills studio for their appointment. Abbi had the whole big hair thing going on. It took a real effort, but she was so proud of her family. Nick too. Philip wasn't happy at all. He was red-faced from crying—that is, until the photographer got out his clown puppet. That did the trick and the pictures came out perfect. "The puppet was scary," Carlee said afterward, "but I was a big girl."

"We're stopping at Baskin-Robbins to celebrate," Nick informed them. Carlee cheered and Abbi playfully joined in.

* * *

Maybe it's in one of his drawers, Abbi thought as she began opening and closing drawers until she found it. The photo was lying on top of Philip's letter. Abbi took the metal-framed picture in her hands and caressed it. Oh, how she longed to hold her baby boy in her arms again, to press her lips to his tender head, to hear his laugh or his cry. She cradled the picture to her and rocked back and forth . . . an ache in her chest. Setting the picture down, she picked up Philip's letter. Her eyes were drawn to a particular portion.

> . . . *I know you did what you thought was best for me and for the ministry, but I just can't live up to what's expected of me. You chose to protect your ministry, but you needed to protect me . . .*

"God!" she cried out, stuffing the letter back in the drawer. "I hate him! I hate him! I hate him! I wish he would have died in that stupid crash!"

Love the whore and trust me.

Abbi froze. The words were unmistakably clear, almost audible, but different from the other voice. This was a still, small, peaceful voice, so startling that Abbi actually turned around to see if anyone was there. Yet she knew the words had popped up out of her own mind. But she also knew they didn't come from her.

Love the whore and trust me.

There it was again. "What does that even mean?" Abbi cried out loud. The instant she asked the question, her eyes were drawn to one of the torn Bible pages where one particular verse seemed to leap out at her—Hosea 3:1: *"The LORD said to* me, 'Go, show your love to your wife again, though she is loved by another man and is an adulteress.'"

Abbi knew the passage. She was well acquainted with the story. She had studied the Bible practically her whole life, even taught a women's Bible study. *This can't be a coincidence,* she thought. *First the words popping in my mind and then this passage.*

Abbi replayed the story of the biblical prophet Hosea in her head. The nation of Israel had been following after other gods, committing spiritual adultery, breaking God's heart. Yet God still loved his people deeply. So much so, that he gave the prophet Hosea an assignment that would be an example of his unconditional love.

God told Hosea to find the prostitute Gomer and marry her. Though it was a tall order, Hosea obeyed. He and Gomer were married and she bore him three children. Hosea was committed to loving his wife, but Gomer betrayed him, cheating and bed-hopping from one lover to the next. Gomer was living with another guy when God ordered Hosea to go get her, bring her home, and love her again.

Tears streamed down Abbi's face as she considered Hosea's plight, how he surely must have felt pain and anger at his wife's betrayal. Yet, in unquestionable obedience, with all the hurt raging in his heart, Hosea went and purchased Gomer, who was on the market as a sex slave, and he brought her home, not to punish her but to love her unconditionally.

Love the whore and trust me. There it was again, a third time, from deep within her core.

"I can't do this, God! I don't love him!" Abbi shouted as she collapsed in Nick's chair exhausted. "I don't want to love the whore!" Abbi knew Nick had never cheated on her. Instead of physical adultery it was emotional. Nick had pursued other passions in his life even though they were associated with ministry. From an outside perspective it all seemed good, but it left him disconnected from his wife and family, which opened the door to a dark broken path.

Something stirring in the hallway caused her to look up. Expecting Deuce, she saw Maria standing in the doorway.

"You okay, Señora Abbi?" asked Maria. "I heard you crying."

"Oh, I woke you," said Abbi, drying her eyes with the back of her hand, embarrassed. "I'm sorry."

On that first day, when the two of them had returned from the hospital, Abbi asked Maria to stay the nights with her because she didn't want to be alone.

"I'm fine," said Maria. "I was awake anyway praying and heard you."

"Something happened, Maria," said Abbi. "I think God just spoke to me. No, I *know* God spoke to me."

"What did he say?" asked Maria.

"I was standing right here when all of a sudden the words 'Love the whore and trust me' popped into my head out of nowhere." Abbi held out the page of the Bible. "Then my eyes fell on this."

Maria took the ragged page in her hand and read. Handing it back she said, "So, you're like Hosea and Nick is like Gomer."

Abbi shook her head. "I know it's crazy," she stammered. "How could God expect this from me?"

"Señora Abbi," Maria said, her expression suddenly one of stern warning, "I think that's something you need to be taking up with God, not me."

"I hate divorce, Maria!" Abbi said in frustration. "You think I want to go through this? I don't, but let's face it, Christians get divorced every day. It happens."

"Sí, it does."

"God forgives divorce."

"Yes, he does," said Maria. "But this is about you obeying God and believing him for your marriage, trusting him with what he has clearly told you."

"What if nothing happens?"

"Obey and leave the results up to God, who is faithful," said Maria.

"What if I don't like the results?" Abbi said quietly, slightly above a whisper.

25

Time in the hospital is strange. When you've been in long enough, the days start to run together and you lose the sense of time. Monday or Friday? I couldn't tell. After Abbi ripped up the divorce papers, I figured maybe there was something to live for after all. Eventually I was taken out of traction and started in-patient physical therapy. I also started eating solid foods and gaining back some of the weight I'd lost.

Once out of ICU and into a regular room, I began getting a steady stream of visitors, but still only those approved by Abbi or me. One day while I was bored watching *The Price Is Right*, the announcer shouted, "Betty Grover, come on down!" Ringing bells and cheers from the studio audience broke out. While Betty was running down the aisle, hands waving in the air, there was a knock on the hospital room door. My mom,

Leona, peeked her head in. "Yoo-hoo," she called out. "Are you awake?"

"Yes ma'am!" I hollered. "Come on in!"

She walked through the door, followed by my brothers, Charles and Cliff, my sister Tessa, and Abbi. Carlee was away at school. The clan had flown in from Topeka and Abbi had put them up at our house. She told them it was a good time to come and wanted it to be a surprise.

It was.

A family reunion of sorts was taking place in my hospital room. Knowing they each had their own set of issues, I was amazed that my siblings were actually able to organize themselves and pull the trip off. I was also deeply touched. What effort and expense it had taken for them to come, all for me, to support me.

They were laughing and carrying on together, having a good ol' time. They definitely didn't have that churchy or religious feel that some of the other visitors had. Two different women from the church had come by, both feeling "led" to pray for me. Somehow they had slipped past Abbi. One had a "word" for me that God loved me but was chastising me, that he could still use me but only if I submitted to his authority. I rolled my eyes. No news flash there. "It's a hard message," she said, "but someone has to give it." The other one had some "godly" advice for me: "Just fall on the grace of God and love him," she said. "If you will only praise him in your pain, he will raise you up." It wasn't that their words were heresy or anything like that. Of course they were true. They were just the wrong words at the wrong time. I really got to see that principle up close and personal. When you're flat on your back from being run over by life and have deep ruts of pain and regret dug into your psyche, your perspective on things changes.

My family, on the other hand, offered no religious talk or judgment. They didn't try to fix me. Instead, they rallied around me. I couldn't believe it. I was sure they would disown me. After all, I was the only preacher in the family and had tried to get them all saved. In the early years of my ministry, I was deep on zeal and shallow on wisdom. I said things and did things that hurt them. Now here I was, the most dysfunctional of them all. Yet they were circling the wagons around me.

"Hey, Nick, you have to see this!" my sister Tessa said, handing me her cell phone, which was playing a video. "Charles is famous. I think he's gonna take your place." They all laughed, except Charles.

"Whatever," he said.

I took the phone and watched as my brother Charles blasted the media in my defense. Some bloodhound member of the press had made the mistake of poking a microphone in his face while he was here in D.C. The press was digging for any new information, any new angle they could exploit.

Charles was five years younger than me, but he looked ten years older. Alcohol and a hard life had taken its toll. With a weathered face, prematurely graying hair pulled back into a ponytail, he took to my defense.

"I don't talk too good," he said taking a drag on his cigarette, blowing a smoke ring. "But it seems to me my brother is about as human as all of us. I can tell you this: Nick Gregory loves God. He's been through a dark time of depression. He'll be back. I believe in Jesus because of him."

I handed the phone back to my sister and wiped my eyes. "Thanks, Charles," I said, seeing my brother in a whole new light. Beneath his hardened shell was a real person with a heart and soul that loved and felt deep pain. He nodded back at me. Charles had struggled with addiction most of his adult life, but he was a believer. I know that for a fact. What I had just gone through gave me a brief glimpse into what it was like not to be able to stop yourself from destructive behavior. Maybe I was an addict, too, just of a different kind. We label addictions as acceptable or unacceptable. Drugs, alcohol, and sexual addictions are taboo, but what about power and abuse? What about pride and religious self-righteousness? We are all sinners, every stinking one of us.

These guys knew me, the real me with all my flaws, yet they still loved me. They accepted me. Were they angry? Yes. Of course they were angry. Were they frustrated with me? You bet. They'd been proud. Now they were embarrassed, not at me, but for me.

I loved them.

I know that Jesus couldn't do any miracles in his hometown because of his kinfolk's unbelief. And I *did* have to get away from my family in order to do what I was called to do, to be effective. But in the end, Jesus' brothers rallied around his cause. The Bible says that after his resurrection, Jesus' brothers were present in the Upper Room praying with those gathered before Pentecost. And Jesus' brother James died as a martyr rather than deny him.

I certainly wasn't Jesus—not even close! But I was grateful for the support of my family.

"I love you guys," I said, looking at Charles with an expression of gratefulness.

"Ugh," he said. "You're not going to hug me, are you?"

My mom got up slowly, as Tessa and Abbi helped her. She walked over to me, bent over the bed, stroked my hair, then kissed my forehead. "I love you, son," she said. "But listen to this old woman." She wasn't smiling. "Pull yourself together. I can't take any more tragic losses in this family." She grabbed a hunk of my cheek and squeezed. "Ya hear me?"

"Yes ma'am," I said.

The room was quiet for a while after that. My older brother, Cliff the agnostic, had the remote in his hands and started flipping through the channels. He'd watched his beautiful wife, Lydia, suffer and die from ALS. Lydia was a believer. In the end, with all her intellect still intact, she was trapped in a body that refused to function—couldn't talk, lift her head, eat without a feeding tube, or dress herself. Finally, she couldn't breathe. Everybody prayed. Abbi and I flew out and anointed her with oil and prayed. A month later, I preached at her funeral. Lydia never lost her faith, but Cliff did. The incident with Philip and now my downfall weren't helping matters any. But he was here and that meant a lot.

A news story on CNN caught his attention. "Sources confirm that another American journalist has been beheaded by Islamic militants in Southern Iraq. In addition, militants boarded a tourist bus in Baghdad and executed twenty-eight non-Muslims."

Cliff turned down the volume. "What kind of a God allows that?" he exclaimed. "Stupid religious fanatics," he mumbled. After a moment of awkward silence he pointed the remote back to the screen and pressed the volume button.

"In other news," said the blonde anchor, "because of the tidal wave of negative press and threats of boycotts by activist groups, Christian and secular bookstores across the nation, as well as most retail discount giants, are pulling books authored by defrocked megachurch pastor and best-selling author Nick Gregory, who is reportedly recovering in a Bethesda hospital after an automobile accident." While she talked, the footage of my now-famous rant played in the background, zooming in on and highlighting Deuce being run over. After the video was finished, the news broke for a commercial. Cliff clicked off the TV.

"Perfect timing," I said, shaking my head in disgust at the media's exploitation of the situation. I turned to Abbi. "You didn't tell me they pulled my books."

"There's a lot I haven't told you."

26

Al Champion, Martin Nichols, and other leaders from the church had made considerable efforts to visit me for prayer and counsel when they got wind that my memory had returned. They felt responsible for my spiritual well-being and were concerned about me stepping out from under the umbrella of authority—their authority, of course. According to them, I needed to go through the proper healing channels for restoration to future ministry. I guess I was in open rebellion because I didn't want to see or hear from any of them. Abbi had her own issues with certain board members, so she was like an iron gate when it came to letting certain people visit, especially since the visits by the two "prophet" ladies.

Jamison had dropped by with his lovely family, and so had Maria, countless times, along with several other friends we considered safe. Carlee had come back to visit a couple of times. Still obviously hurting and distant, at least she was making an effort. I was getting a steady stream of cards and letters from people all over the world, tons of them, mailed to our home. Abbi would collect them and bring them to the hospital. Apparently, though my reputation had been smeared, I still had quite a few supporters out there. Sometimes Abbi, Carlee, or one of the nurses would read them to me. But mostly I read them myself.

Dear Mr. Gregory,

I know you are going through a very difficult season right now. I guess that's why I felt led to write this letter. During one of my layovers, I was feeling depressed about a situation I was going through so I picked up one of your books in the airport bookstore. As I sat reading your words, God's Spirit reassured me that I can depend on him no matter what stands in my way. Thank you so much, and in your own words, "Never give up the fight!"

In Christ,
Bill

Dear Pastor Nick,

I've never written a letter like this before. After seeing the news and all the bad things you are going through, I had to write. I loved your book and wanted to thank you for

helping me feel a sense of hope once more. It made me feel
that normal isn't that far away from me. It made me feel
I was worthy when I thought I was completely worthless.
Please keep writing. Things will get better.

Anna

Letters like that left me feeling humbled. It always amazed
me how God could take some words I scribbled on a page and
use them to touch someone's life. I guess if God can speak
through a dumb donkey then he could use the words of someone like me.

While most of the cards and letters were encouraging and
lifted my spirits, I got hate mail, too, even death threats, mostly
from animal rights activists. They were outraged by the video
of me running over Deuce and used it as an opportunity to
further their campaigns:

You spilled the dog's blood, now your blood should be
spilled! Stay away from the road because we will run you
down! Animals have rights too!

Not to be outdone, I got my share of hate mail from religious whack jobs too.

You're a false prophet!
You are a tool in the hand of Satan!
You are going to hell and taking people with you.

Repent or perish!

Not blessed just cursed!

After rereading yesterday's batch of mail, this particular morning had been quiet. Neither Abbi nor Carlee had come in yet. My extended family was all back in Kansas safe and sound. I'd had no visitors for a while. The media attention had died down and people were moving on with their lives, which suited me just fine.

Fortunately, one of the things that broke up the boredom was my new twice-daily physical therapy sessions. They were painful and intense to be sure, but they got me out of the bed and into a different environment.

I had completed an intense session, and when Stacy wheeled me back into my room, I almost choked on the apple juice I was sipping. Kenny Squires, my longtime buddy from seminary, was sitting there waiting. Apparently he'd flown out from Tulsa to see me. He was one of the few ministers both Abbi and I fully trusted. Authentic inside and out, Kenny Squires was the real deal. I called him my "pastor of writing" because during the process of writing a book if I ever had a question or doubt, he was the first person I'd call. If my writing passed the Kenny Squires test, both theologically and style wise, I knew it was good because he would tell me the truth. If Kenny said it stunk, it stunk. But if he said it was good, then I knew it was good. Another thing about Kenny was there was not even a hint of competition or jealousy. He sincerely celebrated my success, but had always warned me of the perils of power. I guess I should have listened to him more carefully.

"Who let *you* in?" I grinned.

"Hey, man, I had to give the nurse my last twenty," he said, taking off his white Stetson. He rose from his seat, walked to my wheelchair, and got down on one knee so he could be eye to eye with me. "Good to see you, Nick," he said, wrapping his arm around my head and squeezing. "Good things are happing! God's doing a great work!"

"Amen," said Stacy. "That's right!"

I looked at both of them with an expression that clearly said, *What have you guys been smoking?*

Kenny just grinned that silly grin that I'd come to love through the years.

"It's a conspiracy," I muttered.

"You better listen to this man of God, Pastor Nick," said Stacy as she and Kenny helped me out of the wheelchair and into the bed. I was still weak and dressed in my wrinkled hospital gown, two white threads for legs and whiter tube socks. It had been well over a month since I had come out of the coma and I could only stand up for about thirty seconds without help.

"Don't call me 'Pastor,'" I told Stacy. "I'm not a pastor anymore."

"God's callings are irrevocable, *Pastor* Nick," she said. "You of all people should know that."

Kenny looked at me, still grinning. I knew what he was

thinking. *God totally set you up, brother. He gave you Mother Teresa for a nurse.*

"There are a lot of things I thought I knew," I said. "But now . . . I'm not so sure."

"How's the pain?" she asked, adjusting the bed so I could sit up.

"About at five," I said. "I'm okay for now."

"If you need something for pain, just let me know," she said.

"Thanks, Stacy," I said. "I appreciate you."

"Just doing my job, Pastor Nick," she said as she left the room.

"Smart woman," said Kenny, twirling his hat in his hand. He was wearing jeans, a western belt with a big buckle, snakeskin cowboy boots, a white button-down shirt, and a tan blazer. "She's right, you know."

"You always look like Roy Rogers." I smirked.

"Hey, I'm from Tulsa and raise cattle. What'd you expect?"

"My ministry is over," I said, sighing deeply. "The press is crucifying me. The church is shunning me. There are even people out there who want me dead. It's over, Kenny."

Kenny leaned back in his chair. "You're absolutely right!" he said. "*Your* ministry *is* over. Thank God! What a relief! Now you're free to do God's ministry. Ain't that great?" He let out a hearty laugh. "The true ministry that God wants to do through you is just beginning. Yep, God's got an incredible work for you, Nick, a deep work."

"You're starting to annoy me," I said. As much as I loved him, at that moment, I wanted to slap him!

He just couldn't stop grinning.

"Now you're really annoying me."

Serious all of a sudden, Kenny leaned forward in his chair, eyes narrowing. "Tell me something, Nick. Who sustained you after Philip died?" he asked.

"You call this sustaining me?" I replied. "I lost my mind after Philip! That's why all this has happened."

"Aw, poor you," he said. "For crying out loud, take some responsibility! God didn't do this to you. You played a role, you know. And Philip made his own choices too."

"Only because it's you," I snapped, starting to boil, "I'm letting you get away with those comments." Unlike the church ladies who had paid me a visit, Kenny Squires had authority to speak into my life because he'd invested in me over the years.

"It's true and you know it," he said.

"Like I told Stacy, I don't know anything anymore."

"I don't buy that for a second, Nick."

"But I'm losing everything," I spat. "People hate me. I'm a joke!"

"So, now you don't have to worry about what people think," Kenny said, placing his hat back on his head, adjusting it. "Isn't that wonderful?"

"You're enjoying this, aren't you?"

"God's specialty is breathing life into dead situations."

"But I cried out for God to stop me! He didn't."

"He didn't stop John the Baptist's head from rolling either," Kenny said, locking his arms behind his head, stretching out his legs, crossing his boots. "Now, the way I see this thing is, you're still here. And from what I hear, quite miraculously."

"What's left of me," I said, reaching over and picking up a can of Ensure sitting on the tray beside me. Taking in a long slurp, I made a sour face and slapped it back down on the tray.

"You sure are encouraging today," said Kenny.

"You know I'm just venting."

"I know you are, brother."

"You've always been a good person to vent to," I said. "I guess I know you won't judge me."

Kenny smiled. "Hey, you remember back in seminary when we'd buy groceries and then randomly deliver them to the poorest shacks we could find? Remember that one old lady who cried?"

"Yeah," I said softly.

"Remember what she said?"

"How could I forget? She called us her angels. Said she'd just finished crying out to God, asking him to provide food for her family, and then we knocked on the door with four bags of groceries . . . I miss those days," I said.

"Me too," said Kenny.

"What happened?" I asked at the same moment a streak of pain shot through my leg. Grimacing, balling my hands into a fist, I banged my head back on the pillow.

Kenny jumped up to the bedside. "Do I need to call the nurse?"

"No," I said through gritted teeth. "I'm fine. It'll pass."

And it did. As fast as the pain came, it went. I closed my eyes and Kenny settled back in his chair. We sat in silence for what seemed the longest time. No words were needed.

"Kenny," I finally said, "I need to tell you something. It's important. I haven't told anyone this, not even Abbi. When I was in the coma, something happened." He leaned closer. "This is going to sound strange. I didn't see angels or the pearly gates or have a visit with Jesus, but I think I was transported back in time . . ." I paused and waited for a response.

"Go on. I'm listening."

"I'm telling you, this was more real than any dream. It was as real as you and me sitting here right now. But get this: I woke up in ancient Israel, in Mephibosheth's body!"

I was expecting him to call the nurse and report that I had lost my mind, but he was transfixed. "Love that story in the Bible," he said.

"It was like I was him, experiencing what he experienced. It was weird and awful and fantastic."

"Wow."

"Okay, now listen to this. Here's where it gets crazy. Mephibosheth was crippled. My dog, Deuce, is crippled. I'm crippled! All three of us are crippled. That can't be a coincidence."

"Of course not," Kenny said. He took his hat back off and twirled it. "I don't believe in coincidences."

"But it doesn't make any sense," I said.

"Makes perfect sense to me," he said.

"Really? What do you think it means, Kenny?"

"The way I see it, Nick, you and Mephibosheth are just alike."

"Great, just what I wanted to hear."

"Hey, you asked me," said Kenny, flashing his kindly smile again. "But I know you know the rest of the story. After all, you wrote a paper on it."

"You remember that paper?" I asked.

"You made me read the thing before you turned it in to Dr. Henry. How could I forget?"

Another pain shot through my back and legs—this one more severe, causing me to double over.

Kenny jumped up and took my hand. "You're going to get through this, brother," he said. "Let me get that nurse."

"Yeah," I said, grimacing. "That's probably a good idea."

27

"Okay, Pastor Nick," said Stacy. "I guess this is it." She adjusted my wheelchair and then tightened the straps, making sure they were secure. "You ready?"

"Yes ma'am," I said. "Let's roll!" Being in the hospital for two months had kept me relatively isolated from the bloodhounds. Because I figured the press had gotten wind of my release, I wanted to check out at 2 a.m. or 3 a.m., but Abbi was adamant about checking out at exactly 5 p.m., which was weird. She had been acting strange in a lot of ways, so 5 p.m. it was.

Abbi turned to Stacy. "I'm the one you should be asking that question," she said with a mischievous smirk.

"Okay, Mrs. Gregory, are you ready for this?" asked Stacy.

Abbi cut her eyes at Stacy. "No one is ever ready for this kind of thing."

Though I had begun to gain back some of my weight, I was still not much more than a skeleton, my legs dangling from the wheelchair, atrophy having taken its toll. A physical therapist was scheduled to come by the house three or four times a week. And I would have to be brought back to the hospital three times a week for aquatic therapy. At home, Abbi had converted one of the rooms into a therapy/exercise room.

From the lobby, we could see reporters on the other side of the glass waiting outside to get a shot at us. There must have been fifteen or twenty of them lined up. They weren't allowed inside, so that was where we waited. Glancing out the window into the passenger loading zone, I asked Abbi, "Where's Carlee?" She was supposed to pick us up in Abbi's Lexus. But instead of a white Lexus, a white van with tinted windows on the side doors drove up and stopped in front of us. It was clean, but plain—very plain. Carlee waved from behind the wheel.

"What's this?" I asked Abbi.

"I figured if I was going to be hauling you and Deuce around for a while, this would be more practical," she said.

"What happened to the Lexus?"

"It's at home."

"So you just bought a van?"

"Yep," she said. "Somebody has to deal with things."

"Don't you think we should have discussed it?"

"What's there to discuss?" she snapped. "You were out of it

half the time. Besides, it was only thirty-seven thousand. Don't worry. I paid cash."

I shook my head, "All right. I guess."

When the glass doors of the hospital lobby slid open, flashes went off like fireworks and microphones were shoved in our faces. Already exhausted, I kept my mouth shut. Cutting my eyes at Abbi, I thought my plan could have avoided all this.

"Please respect our privacy," Abbi announced cordially but firmly. As we made our way to the van, a reporter stuck her microphone in front of Stacy. "You heard the lady," Stacy said. "Give the folks some privacy!"

Nevertheless, we were pelted with questions.

"What are your plans now?"

"Will you preach again?"

"What about the divorce?"

"No comment," said Abbi.

"Is the dog dead?"

"What about your books?"

"What if there's an investigation?"

If? I thought. I'd assumed there would be an investigation. *You mean there might not be an investigation?*

Abbi slid open the van door. I tried to stand, but I was wobbly. I leaned on the metal crutches that connected to my forearms. Stacy grabbed me on one side and Abbi grabbed my other side, lifted me up, and sat me in the van's seat. At that moment, I had an eerie flash of déjà vu, remembering Gaius lifting Mephibosheth up into the back of the chariot. Stacy hugged me. *I guess I am Mephibosheth,* I thought, as Stacy slid the van door shut.

Abbi hugged Stacy, thanking her, and then shut the passenger door. The three of us waved good-bye to the hospital staff seeing us off as cameras clicked away and Carlee eased through the parking lot toward home.

"Hello, sweetheart," I said from the backseat. "I'm glad you came."

"Hard to say no when your decrepit father needs help coming home from the hospital and you're an only child," she said.

28

Even though Abbi and Carlee were clearly not happy with me, after being locked up for over two months, the drive home was like being set free from prison. All sorts of sentiments ambushed me. More than anything, I was eager to see Deuce. "You think he will remember me?" I asked, my heart pounding out of my chest with anticipation as we turned onto the interstate. "I can't wait to see the little guy."

"He could never forget *you*, Daddy," Carlee jabbed.

"Carlee!" Abbi snapped, "Enough with the attitude, all right."

"She's right," I said. "How could he forget me? I ran him over."

Abbi got quiet and gazed out the window. Obviously something was up with her too. The tension in the van was thick. My coming home was making things harder on her, more personal. I was no longer some guy in a hospital bed she could leave at any time. The weight of responsibility was bearing down on her shoulders. We were going home to whatever was left of our life together. Even after tearing up the divorce papers, she still hadn't kissed me, hadn't said she loved me, and rarely touched me—only when she had to. In fact, she had told me that she didn't love me, and her actions gave me no reason to think otherwise. Abbi's emotional walls were high. When in public she wore her ever-present photo smile, but I knew she was simply going through the motions.

"He'll probably run away when he sees me," I said, bracing myself for the worst.

Abbi let out a sigh. "He's at the vet anyway," she said. "He had treatment and since we were bringing you home, Dr. Conroy said he could stay the night. I'll get him in the morning."

Disappointed, my shoulders dropped. "You're full of secrets today, aren't you? I was really looking forward to seeing him."

"Yeah, well, you can wait another night," she snipped.

"Abbi?"

"What?"

"Thank you."

"For what?"

"Everything."

She turned away and gazed blankly back out the window.

When we turned onto our street, I was surprised and relieved to see that there were only a handful of paparazzi and no protestors.

"Well, this is a welcome relief," I said.

"Maria and I ran them off," said Abbi.

"And Uncle Charles," said Carlee, rolling her eyes.

"Yes, he did," I said softly.

"And after two months Nick Gregory is old news now," said Abbi.

"That's good news," I replied. *Ironic,* I thought, *I've spent so many years trying to get into the spotlight, but now I want nothing to do with it.*

"Hey, Carlee," I said.

"Yeah," she said, pulling in the gate, easing up the drive. I noticed that the downed camellia bush was still lying there. Dead, its leaves had turned brown and some fallen off. It was the beginning of Christmas season, Abbi's favorite time of year. She normally went wild with the decorations starting the day after Thanksgiving, but this year there were no lights, no tree, no decorations. The place seemed as dead as the camellia bush.

"I know we talked about it at the hospital, but I want you to know again how sorry I am about Marshall."

"He's an idiot," Carlee barked. "Like most men. It just showed me his true colors. I'm glad I found out now. He probably would have let me down too."

Ouch.

One thing I knew for sure, someday my daughter would have no problem landing a guy. They would be lined up. She was right. Marshall *was* an idiot.

"Carlee?" I said again.

"Yes?"

"Thank you too."

She ignored the comment and continued up the drive. Instead of going into the garage, Carlee pulled up to the front entrance of the house.

"This is the easiest way in and out for you," said Abbi. About the time she said that, Maria stepped out the front door.

"All right," said Abbi. "Let's get you out of here."

The van was handicapped-accessible, and my seat swirled to the sliding doors for easy access. I was able to put weight on my legs and lift myself out of the seat, but it took Abbi and Maria to get me out the rest of the way and into the wheelchair. Carla had gotten the wheelchair ready while Abbi and Maria assisted me.

Once I was secure, Maria opened the door and I rolled myself inside. Passing through the foyer, the first thing I noticed that was my office door was open. The shattered crystal and torn Bible pages were still on the floor. Two months they had lain there. I shook my head.

"You told me not to clean it," said Maria.

"Yes, I did," I said.

The lights in the hallway that led to the great room and the rest of the house were off. So were the lights in the great room.

The house seemed oddly quiet, especially since Deuce was not there.

As soon as Abbi wheeled me into the great room, Carlee hit the lights.

"Surprise!"

The room was crammed with people! I guessed fifteen or twenty, all personal friends, some of whom had visited me in the hospital. A few were Abbi's girlfriends. Carlee's best friend, Kelsey, was there as well. A banner strung across the room read, *"Welcome Home, Nick!"* Maria had made a cake and there was a table set with all sorts of snacks and soft drinks.

"Welcome home, Nick," Abbi said softly. She smiled warmly, her green eyes inviting. For a moment I thought maybe it wasn't the photo smile.

"You little sneak," I teased.

Everyone gathered around me, patting me, hugging me, offering encouragement and affirmations of love and support. I was somewhere between feeling like a hero who had just scored the winning touchdown and a complete loser all these people were pitying, when I heard a familiar sound. At first I wasn't quite sure.

"Everyone please quiet down a sec!" I said. "Shh."

There it was again, a distinct "Yelp!"

I looked around but couldn't see through all the people.

"Yelp!"

The crowd parted. Across the room from me, in the opening to the kitchen, stood Deuce. He was looking straight at me.

"Yelp!"

Injured the same day as me, he, too, had had two months of recovery time. And, like me, he still looked a mess. Most of his rust-and-white coat had been shaven, making him look very thin, bones protruding. There were still wounds covered by bandages. His two back legs were fastened on a doggie cart with two wheels allowing him to walk around. Seeing him broke my heart. Pain pierced me and tears welled up in my eyes. I was the one responsible. Kenny was right. When was I going to step up to the plate and take some personal responsibility?

"Yelp." Deuce still stood there waiting, unsure. His expression bored a hole in my heart. Would he forgive me, or would he turn and run?

"Here, boy!" I called. Deuce stood frozen. He looked at Abbi as if asking her permission. She said, "Go, boy!" But he still didn't move. My heart sank.

"Deuce, come, boy!" I called again, this time patting my thigh and whistling. At that, Deuce came running as fast as his little front legs could pull his cart. When he reached my wheelchair, he put his paws up on my legs and tried to jump up in my lap but he couldn't make it. A friend standing near picked Deuce up, like Mephibosheth had been picked up, like I had been picked up, and placed him in my lap.

"I missed you so much, boy!" I said, wanting to squeeze him and pat him hard and scratch him vigorously like I knew he loved, but because of his injuries I only caressed him gently. Crawling up my chest, Deuce excitedly licked my arms and face then laid his head on my shoulder. "Deuce, my buddy," I cried. "My little buddy. You came to me! I'm so sorry. Please forgive me."

Lost in the moment, there was nothing but the two of us—Deuce, my friend, my companion. Thank God he was alive and thank God he didn't reject me. There was not a dry eye in the room. Even Abbi had tears streaming down her cheeks. *If Deuce can forgive me,* I thought, *then maybe, just maybe, Abbi can too.*

29

A good while later, after the guests had mingled and begun trickling out of the house, the bell rang indicating someone at the gate. Maria went to see who was waiting. A few minutes later, she escorted a distinguished-looking gentleman to the waning party. He looked around the room and then walked to my wheelchair.

"We need to talk, Nick. It's important," he said.

"Good to see you, too, Frank," I said sharply. Frank Redfield was one of the top literary agents in the world. You name them, he'd represented them—presidents, politicians, professional athletes, coaches, actors, pundits, and big-time preachers like me. A master at spotting undeveloped talent, Frank saw potential in my writing and speaking and took a risk. Said I had a platform that was on the verge of exploding and that he wanted to make it to where everybody knew my name. He was right and he did. Five *New York Times* Bestsellers and millions of dollars later, he called me his "golden egg." The relationship was mutually beneficial.

Frank held out his hand, but before I could grab it, Deuce had already gotten to it, licking it. He'd been sitting in my lap the whole evening, basking in the attention. Instead of shaking, Frank wiped his hand on the napkin he was holding and slipped it into his jacket pocket.

"So you didn't ever come by the hospital," I said, visibly irritated. "After all we've been through together?"

"I'm here now," Frank replied. "Besides, I sent you a card."

"I got it . . . thanks."

"Don't mention it." His brow furrowed and his expression soured. "Have you been watching the news lately?" he said loud enough for the people still mingling around to hear. Abbi turned our way.

"I'm trying not to," I said. "It's too depressing."

"I'll say," Frank said, lowering his voice. "Can we go somewhere private?"

"My office. You know where it is."

Frank wasted no time leading the way.

"Can someone get Deuce, please?" I asked no one in particular. One of the remaining guests picked him up and set him on the floor. I watched him hobble across the room. "I can't believe you still love me after what I did," I whispered and then wheeled myself to the office where Frank had already made himself comfortable in *my* chair.

"It's a mess in here, Nick," he said.

"My life's a mess," I muttered.

Abbi stuck her head in the door. "Is everything okay?"

"Abbi," said Frank, "you may want to be in here for this."

She stepped up behind my wheelchair and braced herself on the handles. Frank motioned to the leather sofa. "You may want to sit down."

"I'm fine right here," she said.

I looked up at Frank. "What's this all about?"

"There's no easy way to say this," he said, his eyes shifting from me to Abbi then back to me. "I take it that you know about a month ago, a certain bookstore chain started pulling your books."

"I saw," I said defensively. "What about it?"

"Well, it had a domino effect. Bookstores everywhere—even the discount retailers—they all pulled your books. There are no Nick Gregory books on the shelves anymore. You can only get them online, and those sites are catching heat now too."

I moaned. "Not even *Peak to Peak*?"

"Nope."

Abbi stepped away from the wheelchair, brushed some of the broken crystal away with her shoe, and dropped down onto the sofa. "This needs to get cleaned up, Nick."

"It gets worse," said Frank.

"Of course it does," I said.

"Your new book that's scheduled to be released this spring has been canceled, and the publisher wants you to return the 1.5 million-dollar advance."

"What?" I said, slapping my forehead. "No way! They made millions off of me!"

Abbi buried her face in her hands.

"There's more," Frank said and waited for us to gain our composure before continuing. "In addition to the advance, they want back the one-third of the advance you were paid on the current book you were writing when all this happened—another 500K."

"That's two million dollars!" I shouted, banging the armrest of the wheelchair with my fists. "They can't do that. The contract says the advance doesn't have to be paid back!"

"There's a broad warranties and representation clause that I'm pretty certain this falls under. You want me to read it?"

"No thank you!" I said. "I know all about those kinds of clauses. Look, Frank, you're my agent! You should have my back! How could you let that slip into the contract?"

"Excuse me?" said Frank. "It's quite standard. And you can't really blame them. They stand to lose millions because of this."

"You should—"

Abbi cut me off. "Stop talking, Nick."

"What?" I snapped back at her.

"You heard me. Stop talking!"

I puffed up like a toad, sulking.

"I wish I had better news," said Frank.

"It's not your fault," said Abbi. "You've been good to us. I hope this is not hurting you too much."

"I'm taking a significant blow," said Frank. "Thankfully, I don't have all my eggs in one basket. Though I admit, Nick Gregory was my golden egg."

"I'm sorry," I said, through clenched teeth.

"Me too," he said. "But it gets even worse."

I dropped my head, shaking it back and forth. "You're joking, right?"

"Believe me, Nick, I wish I were. The publisher is also suing for the books that got yanked. They want additional retribution in the order of seven million dollars—printing costs, marketing, loss of projected sales, etc."

"They can sue on projected sales?"

"I'm afraid they can," said Frank. "Doesn't mean they will win."

"That's nine million! I don't have that kind of cash lying around."

"Their numbers are probably inflated. They'll settle for five or six, if you have a good attorney."

"Five or six! I don't have that kind of cash lying around either!"

"You have assets, Nick, and they know it. Between your cash and homes."

"They can't touch my homes!"

"If they get a judgment against you they can take all your assets until the settlement is paid. They can make your life hell."

"I'll file Chapter 7 bankruptcy."

"I'm sure you will, but they can still take your houses unless you live in Texas."

"Is it too late to move?" I joked. Nobody laughed.

"If we sold the houses, then we could pay them off," said Abbi.

I looked at Frank. "I guess I'm your 'rotten egg' now."

"Expect to get summoned shortly."

"Thanks for the heads-up," I said sarcastically.

"I hope it all works out, Nick," said Frank. "Look, I need to get out of here. I have a flight to catch—New York. Before I go there's one more small detail we need to take care of." Frank pulled out of his jacket a neatly folded one-page contract and a pen. "Can you sign this release form?"

"A release form?" I asked. "What for?"

"Our agent/author agreement."

"What are you saying? You don't want to represent me anymore?"

"What's to represent?" Frank said, setting the paper and pen on my desk, waiting.

"I'm not signing that," I said.

"Just sign the paper, Nick," ordered Abbi.

"All right," I mumbled, then begrudgingly scribbled my name on the release form.

"Thank you," said Frank, taking the contract. He folded it and slid it into his jacket. "I'm sorry about all this. We had a great run." He patted me on the back, gave Abbi a quick hug, and left.

My stomach churned. It felt as if someone had kicked me the gut about fifty times and then left me in a dark alley to wallow in my own vomit. I looked over at Abbi sitting on the sofa. Her head was buried in her hands. How many more surprises like this could she take?

Finally, she stood up. "I have to get back to our guests now," she said and left the room.

Alone in my office for the first time since that morning two months earlier, I observed the Bible pages still strewn on the floor around the broken crystal. Opening my mouth to pray, no words came out, only indecipherable groans.

"I told you it was all coming down, Nikky boy. Ha, ha. What a loser. I told you!"

Just as I was about to give in to despair, Deuce limped in the office and made an attempt to curl up at the foot of the wheelchair. His legs wouldn't cooperate, so he licked my leg instead.

"How can you forgive me, boy?" I said, shaking my head. "How?"

30

Abbi marched down the hall then abruptly changed her pace. She slapped on the photo—good pastor's wife—smile before entering the room where the remaining guests were waiting. She made her way around to everyone, thanking them for coming, explaining that Nick was tired and needed to rest. After saying the proper good-byes, she started nervously picking up.

"I'll get that," said Maria, sensing Abbi was upset. "You rest now."

"Thank you, Maria," said Abbi. "I think I will go lie down."

Maria pulled an envelope out of her apron with Abbi's name on it and handed it to her. "While you were in the office, Laurie gave me this to give you. She had to leave."

Abbi walked to her bedroom, shut the door, and locked it

behind her. Collapsing to her knees at the bedside, Abbi cried out, "God, I can't do this! I need out! Please!" She stayed on her knees rocking back and forth, waiting—hoping for something, a word, a sense of peace, anything. But all she felt was cold nothingness that matched the dead gray sky outside the window.

* * *

Abbi sat down on the bed, opened the envelope, and pulled out the greeting card. On the outside of the card was a picture of a Jack Russell terrier that looked just like Deuce before the accident. His head was tilted, ears floppy, and tongue hanging out. A caption underneath the picture read *"God wruffs you."*

Abbi smiled. Inside was a handwritten note:

Dear Abbi,

I'm not good with words so I'll just tell you. I know that you're hurting. I can't even imagine what you must be feeling right now with all that you've been through beginning with Philip and now Nick. I have no great words of wisdom. Just know I will be lifting you up in prayer every day to our great and faithful God. If you ever need someone to vent on or to just hold your hand, I'm here for you. This afternoon as I was driving to your house for Nick's party, the Lord put this scripture on my heart. I don't know what it means, if anything, but I felt I had to share it with you.

Here goes. "The LORD *said to me, 'Go, show your love to your wife again, though she is loved by another man and is an adulteress'" (Hosea 3:1).*

Your friend,
Laurie

Abbi let the note drop into her lap and clenched both fists. Shaking them in the air, she cried, "Okay, Lord, I get it! I get the message! I want to obey, but this is difficult. I'll stay, but you have to change my heart."

31

Winter blew through, dumping a couple of big snows as it passed. Spring was only a few weeks away, but you'd never know it by the weather. Snow was still on the ground. Not that it mattered to me. I rarely went outside anyway.

For some unknown reason, Abbi did not leave me. Still, the two of us coexisted more like roommates than husband and wife. Except for the times she was assisting me, she stayed on the other side of the house or was out running errands. Sometimes she stayed gone for long periods of time. Clearly, Abbi was struggling and keeping her distance from me. Ten thousand square feet gives a person a lot of space to hide. Despite her decision to stay, Abbi and I were growing apart. Sleeping in separate beds didn't help. Carlee was back in school but chose to come home less and less. Life for me was as cold as the brutal wind whipping in from the Chesapeake Bay.

On top of everything else, Frank's words had proven true. The publisher sued for nine million dollars and was cold and professional about it. The litigation process could have dragged on for months, but because their case was so strong, our attorney recommended that we settle. We settled for six million dollars and they wanted their money. Abbi was right: if we wanted to move on we were going to have to sell our way out. Fortunately, we had assets to cover it and they gave us a grace period in order to liquidate. We would lose practically everything, and I had no prospect of a future. I didn't know what to do. I'd trained my whole life for ministry, but now who would hire a monumental failure like me? Not that I even wanted to do ministry again. Some days, I didn't even know what I believed anymore. But it was useless to even consider that possibility until I had recovered physically.

Oh yeah, there was one other small detail. While we had pretty good health insurance coverage that took care of 80 percent of my medical expenses, the 20 percent left over was turning into a sizable debt. Then there were the attorney fees. The bills just kept stacking up. We could pay off everything, but even with the settlement, there would be barely anything left over. The millions I'd made from writing books was being wiped out basically overnight, and I'd done it all to myself. Not only a cripple, now I was bankrupt financially, emotionally, and spiritually. Nick Gregory officially had nothing left to offer.

The worst part of it all was that my foolish and selfish decisions were hurting all the people I loved. Even Carlee's tuition would be affected. She'd already started working as a server at an upscale restaurant. Thankfully she only had one more semester, but she had counted on pursuing her master's degree. Maybe she could get a scholarship.

There was no need for any voices in my head to tell me how awful I was. If I had died in the crash, everything would have been taken care of. But it was useless to dwell on that failure too.

Since I still held a grudge against God, my prayer life was virtually nonexistent. Much of my time was passed sitting in the recliner or my faithful wheelchair with remote in hand watching movies and football, checking out mentally and becoming more and more depressed. Even my appearance had become sloppy. I rarely shaved or combed my hair, and my breath was nasty. Maybe I was Mephibosheth after all. Maybe that was another reason my wife was keeping her distance.

On this day, Abbi had taken Deuce to the vet and was running some errands. Unusually fatigued that morning, I just sat in front of the tube feeling like my life was wasting away. Sitting there flipping through the channels, the dark cloud of depression descended upon me again. It had become a regular occurrence. I never knew when the depression would hit, but it was always there, hovering in the background, waiting to drop down upon me. When I couldn't take one more rerun of *Family Feud*, I clicked the television off and wheeled myself into my office to look out the window and think. It was snowing outside.

The first thing I noticed upon entering the office was that someone had cleaned it. I know it might be difficult to believe that it would go that many months untouched, but I wanted *no* one in my office and *no* one to clean it! The broken crystal and torn Bible were reminders of that day and fed my depression. But now the whole room was straight, everything neat and in place. The broken crystal on the floor had been swept up and the Bible with its torn pages stacked neatly on my desk. Just like when I snapped in the front yard that day, all the pressure and anger I was feeling came boiling to a head. My office was the one place I had left, a place where I was still in control. Even though it had been a mess, it was *my* mess. I would clean it up when I was ready. Seeing it clean reminded me of how *not* in control I actually was.

"Maria!" I erupted, shouting at the top of my lungs.

Seconds later she came rushing through the office door. "Señor G!" she huffed, out of breath. "Are you okay? What happened? I thought you fell or something!"

I looked at her, seething. "I told you not to clean my office!"

Her shoulders slumped and head dropped. "*Sí*, señor," she said.

"Never touch anything in here again! Do you understand?" I jerked my wheelchair around, back toward her.

"*Sí*, señor."

After Maria left the room, I took the back of my hand and knocked the Bible off my desk, rescattering the pages. Then I turned and stared back out the window. The cold, dreary outside reflected my inside with one exception. Outside was getting whiter while my soul was getting blacker.

"*You're a real piece of work, Nikky boy. You know that? A real piece of work.*"

While staring out the window, I watched Abbi's Lexus turn into the gate and creep up the driveway. *How much longer will she get to drive it?* I thought. *How much longer before she breaks and finally leaves me?*

Spinning my wheelchair, I scooted up to the computer, clicking it on. For what? Habit, I guess. Avoiding social media like the plague, I could always log on to Amazon and see how far my books had fallen or read all the hateful comments. I could go on YouTube and watch my fiasco again and again, read the ridiculous and hateful comments there. The video was up to 107 million views, though in the last month it had slowed to only a million. Crazy. *If only I could get royalties from YouTube views!*

"Yelp!"

I whipped my head around.

Deuce was standing in the doorway, red ball in his mouth, a look of anticipation in his eyes. "Yelp!" His fur was growing back. Almost to his pre-accident state, he no longer needed the assistance of the wheeled cart to pull his hind legs but was left with a permanent limp. Actually, he hopped around on three legs, dragging the one. It was hard to watch, but Deuce didn't complain.

He wants to play? I thought. *How can he possibly think about playing? He's crippled. I'm crippled. Our lives stink.*

"Here, boy," I said, spinning the wheelchair around to face him. He hobbled over to me and dropped the ball at my feet. I bent over as best I could, groaned, picked up the ball, and tossed it through the doorway, down the hall. Deuce did a three-legged dash to retrieve it just as Abbi stepped into the office.

"Nick," she said, noticing the torn-up Bible pages all over the floor again. "What's the deal? I cleaned your office last night!"

"Oh," I said, mentally slapping myself. "You did, huh?"

"Yes," Abbi said with her hands planted firmly on her hips, foot tapping a jillion miles an hour.

"Uh, have you seen Maria?"

"She's in the house somewhere." Abbi tilted her head. "Why?"

Ignoring her, I wheeled through the house, Abbi following me. This was one time I wished she would keep her distance!

"Maria!" I called as I rolled. "Maria!"

"Yes, señor," she said, coming out of the laundry room. She was smiling, but I could tell she'd been crying.

"Maria," Abbi said concern in her voice. "What's wrong?"

"Oh, nothing, Señora Abbi," she said. "I was just praying for you and thinking." She was covering for me.

"I was wrong, Maria," I blurted out. "I'm a total jerk. Please forgive me."

"What'd you do this time, Nick?" Abbi grilled.

"It's okay," said Maria. "Really, it was nothing."

Abbi looked long and hard at me and then Maria. "All right, if you say so," she said, walking away. I suspected she knew there was more to the story.

Maria shifted her gaze to me. "Oh, Señor G, I have already forgiven you," she said without a trace of anger or bitterness in her voice.

"But how?" I asked. "How can you forgive me so easily? You have every right to be angry."

"I'm not angry, Señor G. I'm hurt. But Jesus has forgiven me of so much. How could I not forgive you?" Maria placed her index finger on my heart and poked gently. "Besides, I know the real Señor G is still buried inside and will be resurrected one day."

"I love you, Maria," I said. "I'm going to miss you when this place sells."

"*No quiero hablar de eso,*" (I do not want to talk about it,) she said.

32

"Help! Maria! Nick! Come quick!"

We both heard Abbi's urgent cry from the kitchen. Maria ran ahead while I wheeled behind. By the time I made it to the kitchen, I was panting. Abbi was on her knees, bent over Deuce, caressing him. He was curled up on the floor, eyes open but glassed over, pupils dilated—still, not blinking. He looked dead. The red ball was by his side along with several untouched pieces of his favorite treat. Maria was hunched over, hands on her thighs, praying under her breath.

Abbi looked up. "He's barely breathing," she said. "I called him and he didn't move. At first I thought he was sleeping, then I saw his eyes were open but he wasn't moving. I gave him a treat and he still didn't move. I'm scared! We have to get him to Dr. Conroy, fast!"

Abbi scooped Deuce up in her arms and stood upright. "Maria, please take him while I go get the van," she said to her. "Meet me out front."

Abbi took off and Maria carried Deuce back down the hallway to the foyer and the front door. I was helplessly tagging behind in the wheelchair, strangely out of breath. My heartbeat seemed different, irregular. I had been pushing myself hard during therapy sessions, but my heart had never fluttered like this. Stopping at the front door, my thoughts shifted away from me when I saw Maria outside standing in the covered drive waiting and praying.

"Oh, *Santo* Jesus, cover Deuce with your Spirit. Keep him, Lord. Heal him. God, you love our pets. You create Deuce for purpose, *gracias,* Jesus—to bring healing and comfort to this family during this difficult time. Now I'm asking you to bring comfort to Deuce, Lord—" Maria stopped midsentence as the van whipped up to her side. Abbi leaned over, opened the passenger door, and Maria slid onto the seat with Deuce limp in her lap.

I pushed myself up to Maria's door and asked, "What can I do?"

"Sorry, Nick," said Abbi. "Just pray this dog doesn't die!"

Maria gave me a sad look and shut the door.

"Be careful. The roads are slippery," I mumbled under my breath as they drove away. Sitting there, I watched Abbi drive out the gate as fast as the snow and slush would allow her. Thankfully, the protestors had given up weeks ago. The snow and bone-chilling wind had helped keep them away. "God," I prayed, "protect them. Be with Deuce. Please, whatever is wrong with him, don't let him die." The residual effects of my foolish choices were still hurting those I loved. "God, I deserve your punishment, but not Deuce, please."

"Yes, you do deserve it, Nikky boy. You're just a dead dog, and Deuce is going to die too!"

33

No sooner had Abbi's van turned the corner and faded out of sight, than a black Corvette pulled up to the gate and buzzed to be let in.

Shoot! It was physical therapy day. With everything that had happened that morning, it had totally slipped my mind. I whipped my wheelchair around, back into the foyer, and pushed the button on the wall to open the gate. Ray, my muscle-bound PT guy, drove in. If reincarnation were true, I'd be convinced that Ray had been a medieval torture expert in his past life. His job was to push, pull, contort, and bend me past the limits of human possibility until I nearly passed out. He was gifted in zeroing in on previously unknown areas of my body where he could inflict as much pain as possible. He apparently enjoyed his job.

"Good morning, Nick!" he said, jovial as always. The first few sessions he'd insisted on calling me Mr. Gregory to be professional and respectful, but his politeness grew nauseating. Then I'd begged him, "Please, call me Nick."

"Yes sir, Mr. Nick," he said.

"Just Nick will be fine."

The two of us had become pretty close, my torturer and me. How can you not be close with someone who does all those unnatural things to your body, pushing you so hard that you want to punch him?

"I've got great news!" he announced, guiding me through the house toward the converted therapy room. With his green scrubs, bronze tan, wavy blonde hair, and South Pacific blue eyes, it was hard not to like the guy. He had a natural charisma and self-confidence.

"Let me guess," I said. "You're engaged to a supermodel?"

"Ha." He laughed, flashing a smile. "No way. I haven't had that date with Carlee yet!"

"You'd better step up your game! She doesn't impress easily."

"Hey, I'm up for a good challenge!" he replied, patting my back.

Being with Ray made me long for Philip and the father-son connection we would never know again. "So, what's the good news?" I asked.

"We're going to get rid of that wheelchair today!" he said. "Isn't that great? I want you to stop depending on it. From now on, you're gonna use a walker or crutches."

I grimaced, thinking, *I'm sure that's gonna be great for you.* I knew what I looked like when attempting to walk—weak and broken, wobbly-kneed and clumsy. On top of that, it was painful.

"You'll thank me later," said Ray. "Remember what the doc told you. That if you work hard, within a year you won't even need crutches, possibly only a cane."

"You're killing me, Ray," I said.

"Your success is my success," he said. "Hey, man, where's your little buddy? He's usually right by your side. He's like the canine version of you, man."

Physically Deuce is like me, I thought. *That's about as far as the similarities go. His spirit, character, and unconditional love far surpass mine.* "I should have told you," I said. "Abbi rushed him to the vet just minutes before you drove up. I'm surprised you didn't see the van."

"Really?" said Ray. "He okay?"

"It's the strangest thing," I said. "Deuce has been doing so well. His spirits have been up. If it weren't for the crushed leg and hip, he'd practically be his old self. This morning, one minute he was playing with his ball, the next minute he was flat on the floor like he was dying. I'm worried, Ray."

"Wow, Nick, I'm sorry. Do you want to reschedule this session? I know the little guy is important to you."

"Yeah, you can say that again. I can't imagine life without him around."

Ray looked at me, waiting for a response to his question.

"No," I said. "Let's just get it over with while they're gone. Besides you're here already and it'll keep my mind occupied."

"Okay then," he said. "Let me get those vitals."

He put the blood pressure cuff on my arm, pumped it up, and did his count. Then he held my wrist and looked at his watch. Ray placed his stethoscope to my chest, listening to my heart.

He sat back with a concerned look on his face. Then he retook my vitals, which was a first.

"Everything okay?" I asked.

He held up his finger for me to not talk. A moment later, he removed his stethoscope. "Something's not right, Nick," he said. "Your pulse is too slow. Rhythm is off. Have you had trouble breathing? Been fatigued?"

"I haven't felt right since we found Deuce in the kitchen. I had trouble catching my breath, and my chest felt kind of funny. It's happened a couple of times lately."

Ray's carefree attitude was gone, replaced with a sense of urgency. "Nick, we need to get you to the hospital, ASAP."

"No problem," I said. "I'll make an appointment and Abbi can bring me in later today or this week."

"No, Nick," he said. "You're not hearing me. You have to go now. Like, right now. I'm calling an ambulance."

"You're serious?"

"As serious as a heart attack," Ray said. "You don't play around with these things." He picked up his cell to call the ambulance.

"Can't you just take me in?"

"Protocol. My job requires it."

"Did I have a heart attack?"

"No sir, but if you don't get medical attention, you will have one. And that's a guarantee."

Something in my gut told me that I was going for an extended stay. *Wonder how much this is going to cost.* While waiting for the ambulance to arrive, I texted Abbi, *"FYI, Ray said I needed to go to the hospital for tests. Probably no big deal. Don't worry. Ambulance is just a precaution."* I didn't want to cause her any more distress than she was already under. I pushed Send and waited.

There was no response.

34

Ray helped me pack a few necessities. He was trying to keep me calm and my heart rate down. Less than fifteen minutes later, the paramedics were lifting me into the ambulance. They moved me from the wheelchair to the stretcher, treating me as if I'd suffered a massive heart attack. As they slid me into the ambulance, Ray gave me the thumbs-up and they shut the ambulance door.

"Maybe this is really it, Nikky boy. It's what you want anyway. Just think. You might be seeing Philip today."

Riding to the hospital and hearing the sirens scream, something was different. Before, I had been depressed and wanted to die. Now I was still depressed, but I wanted to live. As much as my relationship with Abbi and Carlee was strained, all I cared about was my family and those who loved me, including my little buddy. Maybe the voice was right. What if this was it? Maybe my chances were all up. Had I been given another shot and was now out of time? There was so much I needed to say to Abbi and to Carlee. So much left undone. I had to make things right for them.

This time I didn't want to bail on them. I wanted to see things through until they were set and I could move on without any regrets or guilt. And Deuce, what if he died? It would kill Abbi.

No . . . no, please! My chest squeezed with anxiety. I could feel my heart fluttering, panic setting in. About that time the monitor I was hooked up to made a high-pitched beeping sound. The paramedic working frantically over me started spinning and then everything went black . . . again.

35

When I came to, I found myself facedown and prostrate on a cool, marble floor, my arms stretched out before me. I knew exactly where I was because I could smell the stench of Mephibosheth's body—my body.

"כלב מת אוהב אותי." (Dead dog like me.) The Hebrew words rolled off my tongue in a faint whisper, and again I could sense it was Mephibosheth speaking. "Dead dog like me."

A hand touched the back of my shoulder. Expecting a sword, I instinctively recoiled in fear, then realized it was a soft, comforting hand . . . patting me.

"Please don't execute me," I begged, still facedown, speaking low, hopelessness in my voice. Standing somewhere near me, Ziba let out a snicker.

"Mephibosheth." The voice was soft and compassionate,

like the hand, yet spoken with clear authority. "Look up." The hand reached down and clutched mine. Turning my head, I saw a gold signet ring on one of its fingers as it pulled me up to my knees.

It was King David.

He had left his throne, walked down the steps, and was kneeling on one knee at my feet. My weary, pain-filled eyes met the king's. Like the sharpest sword piercing the hardness of my outer shell and reaching deep into the sinew of my soul, his eyes were filled with truth and grace, not the harsh judgment I was expecting. King David kissed the top of my dirty, stinky head. "Mephibosheth!" he said, kindness in his voice. "Don't be afraid. You are home now."

"Here am I, my king," I said, looking up from my knees, my mind trying to absorb what had just occurred. I was expecting death, but the king was showing undeserved grace and mercy.

"Take my hand," the king said, holding out his. My grimy, disgusting hand clutched his and he pulled me up and into his embrace. "Mephibosheth! Jonathan's son!" There were tears in his eyes.

I stooped in honor.

"Get this man a chair," King David ordered Ziba as he walked back up the steps and stood by his throne. No longer a young man, David still had a youthful ambience about him, yet he was weathered and creased by battles fought.

Ziba let out a huff of irritation and then scrambled to get

the exquisite bronze chair that was covered with exotic carving. He placed it down next to me without even acknowledging I was there. Aware that every eye in the room was fixed on me, I wrestled myself to my feet, holding the chair for support, and then stood waiting for the king's permission to sit.

After a moment, David motioned with his hand for me to be seated as he lowered himself on the throne, a throne that wasn't at all what I'd envisioned it to be. More like an extra-large love seat, it had silk pillows on top of animal skins—bear and lion. Leaning against it was a bow with a quiver of arrows, a military shield, and a spear, making it look like a warrior's seat rather than a king's throne. A primitive leather sling and five smooth stones were prominently displayed like a game ball on a shelf. Saul's golden cup was on a table next to the throne.

Waiting for King David to speak, I took in the scene around me—a curious blend of majesty and elegance mixed with the roughness and strength of a warrior. And then there was me, Mephibosheth—crooked, filthy, and weak, sitting in this magnificent chair, not executed as I had anticipated but kissed and embraced by the king. Who would have imagined?

Those standing in the room began chattering among themselves. David motioned for silence, indicating that he was about to speak. He rose to his feet, gazing down at me from his throne. "Mephibosheth!" he said again, his voice echoing throughout the chamber.

"My lord," I replied, bowing my head.

"For the sake of the covenant I had with your father, I sought you out to bestow upon you the kindness of God."

The sound of chattering filled the room again.

"Silence!" the king thundered, holding up his hand. When the room had quieted down, he eased back down on the throne and closed his eyes as if he were reaching back for some long-ago memory. Reopening them, he said, "Let me tell you a story about your father. Jonathan and I made a covenant of friendship to one another. I loved him as my own soul. He was a loyal, honorable man, closer to me than a brother and a pillar of support in battle. I trusted him with my life. When I was in hiding and evil was being planned against me, your father devised a clever plan to save me from certain death.

"After three days of hiding, he signaled me by way of bow and arrow whether I was to come out of hiding or to flee. If he had not come through for me, I surely would have fallen into evil hands. Your father was a valiant warrior, but he had a tender heart for the Lord and for his friend. Now I have finally found you so I can save you and fulfill my promise to your father." King David wiped his eyes and walked back down the steps. Kneeling at my side, he draped his arm around my shoulders. "I love you, my son," he whispered into my ear. Then he stood up straight, his hand still on my shoulder, and shouted to everyone in the room. "From this day forward, Mephibosheth shall eat at my table!"

The room erupted in cheers, except for Ziba. He was fuming.

"And all the land that belonged to your father, Jonathan, and your grandfather, Saul, I now restore to you." David turned to Ziba. "And my servant Ziba here, I give to you. He and his servants are now your servants."

"But, my lord and king," I whispered, "I am not worthy of such a gift."

David didn't respond. His attention was still focused on Ziba, whose face had reddened, his expression one of disdain, the veins bulging out of his head.

"Ziba, your bitterness has consumed you like leprosy," said the king. "You have much to be grateful for. I saved your life from certain death, remember."

Ziba bowed. "Yes, my lord. I am forever in your debt."

"Good," said David, turning back to me. "All that is required of you is to accept my offer and come to my table. Will you accept?" David held out his hand.

Wiping the wetness from my eyes with the back of my hairy, crusty hand, I said, "What is your servant, that you should notice a dead dog like me?"

"Enough of this 'dead dog' rubbish!" he said. "Mephibosheth! You are no dead dog. Goliath was a dog! You are royalty! Though crippled and broken, you will always be royalty. Do you accept my offer?"

I bowed. "Yes, my king, I accept. I, too, owe you my life."

David laid his hands on the top of my head. "The Lord be praised," he prayed. "Let your mercies, O Lord, be upon us. You are our hope and our shield, our help in time of need.

Thank you for bringing Mephibosheth, my son, back home! May he live in peace all his days. We magnify and exalt your holy name."

I felt as if a warm blanket of anointing oil had been poured over my head and was running down my body. Threads of brokenness in my heart were coming together and being healed. This king—this man after God's own heart—had touched me and prayed over me as if I were his own. David did not abandon his promise to his friend. God would not abandon me even when I didn't deserve it and had nothing to offer in return.

Something happened.

Though still broken and twisted on the outside, my insides were being cleansed. I felt like I was a new man and had a place at the king's table. I was royalty. I had a family. I was a son.

David clapped his hands. "Get this man a bath!"

36

"God must *really* have something for you to do," said Dr. Toler. He had his clipboard in hand, head down, reviewing my chart. I was sitting up in bed feeling chipper. I felt great, both physically and emotionally—better than I'd felt since I could remember. Instead of terror, this time I had awakened from my trip back in time filled with peace—an unexplainable peace, a peace that passed my understanding.

"If you hadn't been in that ambulance," Dr. Toler continued, "you'd be dead." He pulled a chair next to the bed and sat down. "Nick, you *were* dead—you flatlined for thirty-one seconds."

"Really?" I said, scratching my head. "Like 'dead' dead?"

"Yep, dead. As far as this life goes, the fat lady had sung."

"Only thirty-one seconds?" It felt as if my time before King David had been at least an hour.

"Thirty-one seconds is too long in my book," said Dr. Toler. He smiled and patted my arm. "The paramedics brought you back. And Ray, your PT, saved your life too. You should throw them a party."

"You're right about that, Doc."

"Can you sit forward? I want to listen to your heart. See if we can get you out of here by this afternoon."

"That quick?"

"I don't see why not," he said, taking his stethoscope and placing it on my heart. "Getting a pacemaker is a relatively simple procedure. These days, it's practically outpatient if there are no complications. In your case we needed to observe you overnight." He was quiet a moment while he listened. "Take a deep breath and exhale."

I drew in a breath and blew it out slowly.

He nodded his head. "Again."

I inhaled and exhaled.

"Your heart sounds strong now."

"I feel great!"

"I bet you do. Your heart's not working overtime any longer."

"Explain it to me again," I said.

"The trauma on your heart from the accident created a stress pressure point, which in turn caused *myocardial weakness*—the weakening of the heart muscle, in your case the left ventricle. This leads to congestive heart failure, which is what you experienced. It's similar to any other muscle that becomes damaged. It has to build back up. The good news is you *can* build it back up. The pacemaker will help your heart until the muscles are back to normal. Think of it as crutches for your heart. The difference being, the pacemaker actually makes your heart function more efficiently."

I smiled apprehensively.

"No need to worry, Nick." He patted my arm again. "With that device inside you, your heart is actually better than new. That's why you feel so great. You won't even know it's in there. These things go for years with very little maintenance. By the time this one wears out your heart may have corrected itself."

"That's great, Doc. I'm so thankful. But I wonder, why didn't you guys catch this earlier?"

"Sometimes it takes a while for the effects of this kind of pressure to show. Think of it like a weak spot on one of your car tires. You don't see it but it's there and the pressure is building. Each time you drive your vehicle it's weakened a little bit more. Then one day, *bam!* There's a blowout. Your vitals hadn't indicated anything abnormal until Ray took them yesterday. This is why we insist on taking vitals before every PT session."

"Makes sense to me," I said.

Leaning forward, Dr. Toler said, "Nick, I want to reiterate something. Most people who go through the trauma you did are either dead or in a vegetative state. So like I said, you must have a reason for being here. You should really think about that."

"Thanks, Doc," I said, already pondering my two episodes as Mephibosheth and all they could possibly mean.

"Don't thank me," he said. "Thank God."

Dr. Toler was right. I'd been given yet another opportunity, just like Mephibosheth had. Living through that moment in his body was surreal. Something happened that I'd never experienced before. I had a peace that didn't reflect the circumstances I was in. My life was broken. My body was broken. My marriage was broken. I was guilty of things. And just when things were at their worst, the King of grace and peace breathed life into my situation. Things were still broken, but I now saw a flicker of hope at the end of the dark tunnel. It gave me the strength to push through this season. I thought about my brother Charles struggling with his addiction, how he'd been fighting it one day at a time, for years, and was still fighting it. That's the place I was at now, taking life one day at a time.

In Mephibosheth's day people took their covenants seriously. King David had searched for a relative of Saul to bless for the sake of his covenant friend, Jonathan. That blew my mind. God had a covenant with us through Jesus' blood. God loved me and wanted me to eat at his table, not because of my performance but because of Jesus. Like Mephibosheth, I was wobbly and weak-kneed with nothing to offer. But God still wanted me. All he required of me was to receive his generous gift and humbly eat at his table. Of course, this was no new revelation to my mind. I'd preached it and written about it for years. But now I really got it in my heart and was experiencing it on a whole new level. Hearing about the grace of God when you're strong and in control isn't the same as hearing it when you are broken, weak, and needy. That's when you see your true condition before God and realize your desperate need for his mercy.

A fresh vision flashed through my mind of Abbi and my marriage covenant with her. My main ministry outside a relationship with the King had always been to love her like Jesus loved me and laid down his life for me. That was how I needed to love her and search out a way to bless her.

Later that afternoon, it was time for me to check out after spending just one night in the hospital. Abbi and Carlee came up to the room. Carlee was home for a few days. There was tapping on the hospital room door.

"Knock, knock." It was Nurse Stacy from the ICU, pushing an empty wheelchair.

"What are you doing here?" asked Abbi, giving her a hug. "Good to see you, Stacy!"

"When I heard Mr. Gregory was here, I pulled some strings so I could check him out."

"Good to see you, Stacy," I said, sitting up in the bed.

"Looking good, Pastor Nick!" she said, squeezing me around the shoulders. Pushing away from me, her eyes narrowed. "Okay . . . what's up? There's definitely something different about you."

"Two words, Stacy," I said. "*Mercy* and *grace*."

"We all need that," she said, patting the empty wheelchair seat. "Now, get in!"

"I'll go get the van and pull it around," said Abbi, shooting out the door.

Nurse Stacy and Carlee pushed me to the elevators, where we rode down to the first floor. Abbi and the van were already waiting. This time I stood on my own and helped myself into the van.

37

Maria was standing in front of the house, waiting with my wheelchair. She wasn't even wearing a jacket. She didn't need to today in this fickle D.C. weather. It was snowing when she and Abbi had rushed Deuce to the vet a day earlier. Now the sun was out and it was in the midfifties.

"Welcome home, Señor G," Maria said warmly, sliding the van door open. Carlee had ridden up front with Abbi. Maria scooted the wheelchair next to the open door. She was looking at me like something was smeared all over my face. "Something's different about you," she said. I suspected she knew.

"Thank you, Maria," I said, sitting down. About that time, I heard a familiar, wonderful sound.

"Yelp! Yelp!" Deuce came run-limping through the front door, his tail wagging at lightning speed, head tilted, showing his teeth. I think he was actually smiling. Happy to see me, he tried to leap into my lap, but still couldn't quite make it. He got about halfway up my legs and started to fall backward. I caught him and pulled him up into a tight bear hug, him licking my neck and face.

He was fine! Deuce was fine! Abbi said he'd had a serious reaction to some new medication that caused the weakness and lethargy. Evidently chasing the red ball as hard as he did led to the little fellow's collapse. Dr. Conroy promptly countered the medication and pumped Deuce with IV fluids until he began to return to normal.

"I'm glad to see you, too, Deuce!" I said, kissing his head, pressing my cheek to his, squeezing. "You're so good, boy! Yes, you are. I love you too!"

"Yelp!"

"There's no question how he feels about you, Nick," added Abbi. She was right. We had bought the dog for Abbi, but Deuce had become my bud.

"It's pretty amazing how he could forgive me of so much and then act like it never happened."

"Amazing grace is what it is," said Maria. "That dog is trying to teach us all something. God forgives our past and never brings it up again. Now, the enemy, that's a whole different story. He's always throwing the past back in our faces. 'Past, shut up!' That's what I tell that liar."

"I don't know. Dogs have short memories," said Abbi, sounding unsure.

Carlee started Googling something on her phone and then said, "Listen to this, Mom. 'The memory of dogs is more humanlike than previously thought. Dogs possess what's known as declarative memory, which refers to memories of specific events that can be consciously recalled.' So when Deuce sees Dad, he remembers."

"Hmm," Abbi said.

"Okay," I said, slapping my thighs. "Since we are all here, I have an announcement to make."

38

"It's really not that big of a deal," I said. "But from now on I'm *not* using the wheelchair. Ray said it's time to wean myself. He's right. It may not be pretty, but I believe God wants me moving forward."

"*God* wants you to?" asked Abbi. "I thought you and God weren't on speaking terms."

"He's been speaking, but I haven't been listening. It's time to start again."

She looked at me, hard. I knew the look—unconvinced.

"Carlee, will you please get the walker out of the back of the van?" I asked. We had brought it home from the trauma center weeks ago, but never took it out. Carlee readily obeyed and unfolded the walker in front of me. After letting Deuce down from my lap, I struggled to my feet, situated myself behind the walker, and the five of us stepped into the house.

Shuffling along, pulling myself, foot dragging behind and raking across the floor, I was reminded of Mephibosheth limping through the palace. Deuce hobbled alongside me, dragging his lame foot too. We were a pair. He looked up, tail wagging, tongue dangling. I stopped to rest.

"Yelp!" Deuce barked, looking up at me, smiling. "Yelp!" Then he started to run-limp ahead of me, glancing back just like he'd done the morning he saved me from killing myself. Deuce was encouraging me to keep going. The dog was encouraging me!

"I'd like to be alone for a while," I said. Abbi, Carlee, and Maria started walking away, but Deuce stayed by my side. "It's okay, buddy, you can stay." He followed me into my office. Closing the door I sat in my chair and Deuce sat awkwardly at my feet. The Bible and pages from my latest outburst were still strewn across the floor. I thought about how I'd unleashed on Maria and was ashamed.

Slowly standing back up, I balanced myself on the desk. Shifting my body sideways, I side-shuffled to the bookshelves. I knew what I was looking for. Lying flat on the very top, gathering dust, was an old leather briefcase I hadn't opened in years. It was the kind nobody uses anymore, with the round bronze buttons you slide and the latches that flip up.

I stretched as high as my contorted body would allow. For

a brief moment, I'd forgotten how bent and damaged I was. In the past, I merely stood on my tiptoes, reached up, and pulled it down. That was how it had gotten up there in the first place. Now, when I tried to stand on my tiptoes and stretch, my withered legs trembled, leaving me about six inches short. I considered calling Maria or Abbi to reach it for me. Instead, I foolishly pulled a couple of thick hardbound books off the shelf, a Bible dictionary and a *Strong's Concordance*, and let them drop to the floor. Using my foot, I positioned the books to where I could stand on them. But getting my foot up there proved more of a challenge than I first anticipated. *This ain't gonna work.* Again, instead of calling Maria or Abbi to help, I scanned the office for something I could use to pull down the briefcase. *The umbrella in the corner—that might work!* With the aid of my walker, I retrieved the umbrella and negotiated myself back in front of the bookshelf. The ceiling to my office was twelve feet high and the top shelf was almost nine feet, so reaching up with the umbrella, I still had to stretch to make contact with the briefcase. Using the hook of the umbrella, I managed to catch the briefcase handle just enough to pull it down.

Unfortunately, it was heavier than I had remembered, much heavier. With my frail legs the weight of the briefcase threw me off balance, and I tumbled to the ground with a loud "thud." Both Maria and Abbi heard the noise and ran into the room.

"What happened?" Abbi asked.

I looked up from the floor, a silly grin on my face, and shrugged my shoulders. "I needed my briefcase," I said.

"Not smart," Abbi said, not amused.

"I agree," said Maria, reaching down to assist me up.

"No thanks," I said, pushing my body into the sitting position with my back resting against the bookshelves. "I'm going to stay down here awhile."

Deuce licked my arm. After placing the briefcase in my lap, I brushed off the dust and flipped open the latches.

39

After I opened the briefcase, once I got past the musty smell, a wave of nostalgia washed over me. Inside were stacks of papers with old typewritten print, whole sentences blotted with Wite-Out, spiral notebooks crammed with doodles, journaling, and study notes from my early years as a Christ follower. Some were sermons and chapters to books I'd started writing my senior year in high school, when I was convinced God had called me to be a writer and a minister. My humble beginnings in ministry were in that briefcase.

I'd gotten a scholarship to play football in college. Big-time coaches had visited my house. Everyone was excited. Parties were thrown. After all, I'd given my whole life to playing football. For as long as I could remember, it had been mine and my dad's dream. At the start of my senior year, Dad told me he'd give me one hundred dollars for every touchdown I scored. His offer must have worked, because I scored twenty-two touchdowns that year!

That same year, after my scholarship offer, I informed my dad that I felt God had called me to ministry and writing. I was ultra-serious. Looking back, that's probably the last thing a father wants to hear his son say, especially when the son has a full-ride football scholarship. But to his great credit, my dad never belittled or shamed me. He simply said, "Nick, if God really called you, then he will continue to reinforce that call. You have a full scholarship. That's God, too, because we can't afford to send you to college. Here's my proposition; take advantage of this opportunity to play football, and if after you graduate you still feel called, I'll support you going to seminary and will help in any way I can."

I thought that sounded pretty fair, so off I went to play football. Since I felt God had called me to write, I majored in journalism. I'm sure Dad thought I would outgrow the writing call, that it was just another one of my momentary whims. But the passion for writing never waned; it only grew stronger. Four years later, I was more sure of my call than ever. God used those four years to develop my writing skills. He also used my time playing football to prepare me for the discipline of ministry. Living in the dorm with the athletes, starting Bible studies, seeing teammates come to Jesus, even baptizing some of them in the training room whirlpool! It was all part of God's plan. And I never stopped writing. Back then I was sure God had called me, but now, after the absurd success it was all over. I'd blown it. Dad was alive to see my success. He died a few years later. While I missed him greatly, I was glad he wasn't here to experience the grief of losing Philip and seeing my failure. Then again, maybe he did see it.

Sorting through the myriad papers, I found what I was searching for. On the very bottom was my seminary paper on Mephibosheth. After retrieving the fifteen-page thesis held together by a rusted paper clip, I set the briefcase aside and began to read its yellowed pages.

The Victorious Limp

A Biblical Story of Brokenness Interrupted
by Outrageous Grace

by
Nick Gregory

Dr. Henry
Old Testament Survey 301
2/19/89

The title alone caught me a bit off guard. *"The Victorious Limp"? Could a limp, being crippled, actually be described as victorious?* It's one thing to write about it, but now I was living it. *Note to self: Be careful what you write.*

"Mephibosheth—a peculiar crippled man whose story is

tucked away, almost hidden, in the vast archives of the Old Testament."

As I scanned the fifteen pages, statements I'd written so long ago seemed to leap out at me and speak to my very situation.

Does the pain from past events and circumstances seem to keep you from being the person you know you were meant to be, the person God created you to be?

Is it hard for you to shake that nagging voice continually telling you that you're not good enough and that God is disappointed in you?

Have you failed God or yourself so many times that you're at the point of giving up?

This guy Mephibosheth was a messed-up dude. When he looked down at himself in the river, he didn't merely dislike the reflection staring back, but he despised it. It repulsed and nauseated him. He wanted to get as far away from himself as possible. The problem was, wherever he went, there he was. How does someone get to that point— the point of seeing themselves as a dead dog?

Mephibosheth had royal blood pumping through his veins and was an heir to the throne of Israel. His dad was Prince Jonathan and his grandfather was King Saul. The guy who grew up to see himself as a dead dog was actually born to rule and reign, to govern a nation and make important decisions, to be respected and honored. Mephibosheth was supposed to be a person of significance,

*not a dead dog. Isn't that us, or at least most of us? We see
ourselves as insignificant creatures living the polar opposite
of what we were born to be—what we were created to be.*

I couldn't believe I'd actually written what I was reading.
There had to be some link between me traveling back in time,
experiencing the life of Mephibosheth, and my writing this paper. Maybe God in his foreknowledge had me write it, knowing it would be the story of my life too. Scratching Deuce behind the ears, I continued to read.

*The central narrative in the story of Mephibosheth comes
from just thirteen verses in 2 Samuel 9 and one verse in
2 Samuel 4 and is the chronicle of a ruined, broken, crippled man with nothing to offer and zero hope. Stuck in an
impossibly deep rut that circumstances out of his control
had carved for him, Mephibosheth was laboriously going
through the motions of his dreary and uncomfortable ex-
istence simply waiting to die. But then one day when he
was expecting the worst, something amazing and radical
happened. God interrupted the desolation of his life with
an outrageous offer of grace. It was an offer that changed
Mephibosheth's whole life. It can change yours too.*

*The end of the story says, "And Mephibosheth lived in
Jerusalem, because he always ate at the king's table; he was
lame in both feet." It was a victorious limp.*

Letting the papers fall into the briefcase, I stared across the room contemplating the words I'd just read. God was extending that same offer to me.

"No, he's not, Nick. God could never forgive you. Not after all you've done, not after Philip."

"I've had it with you," I said in a surprisingly calm voice. "Leave, in the name of Jesus!" Instantly, a peace filled the room.

I should have done that long ago!

Though I was crippled in many ways, the King still wanted me to eat at his table. God wasn't asking me to change or fix myself before coming. He just wanted me to come. But could I accept the gift the way Mephibosheth had accepted King David's offer? Or was I too prideful, too pitiful? Mephibosheth had said yes, yet he remained crippled in both feet. In his brokenness he still had to humbly hobble to the king's table daily for bread. He limped, but it was a victorious limp.

I looked down at Deuce. His head was resting on my thigh. I had accepted his forgiveness. I could accept God's forgiveness, but could I forgive myself?

40

Instead of trying to put the briefcase back on the top shelf, I just left it on the floor and slid it between the bookshelf and my desk. Still sitting on the floor, I again observed the Bible, its pages scattered around me. One by one, I began gathering them up. Once collected, I straightened the pages, slid them neatly inside the Bible, and placed it on my desk.

Using my walker, I pulled myself to my feet and then dropped my body down into the chair. Reaching into one of the desk drawers, I pulled out a roll of clear tape and began taping the pages back into my treasured Bible. With each page, surges of cleansing and renewal moved through me. A shift was taking place. As I taped, I read some of the scriptures. *"He does not treat us as our sins deserve or repay us according to our iniquities. For as high as the heavens are above the earth, so great is his love for those who fear him; as far as the east is from the west, so far has he removed our transgressions from us. As a father has compassion on his children, so the* LORD *has compassion on those who fear him; for he knows how we are formed, he remembers that we are dust"* (Psalm 103:10–14).

On the next page that I taped, I saw, *"Wash away all my iniquity and cleanse me from my sin. . . . Create in me a pure heart, O God, and renew a steadfast spirit within me. . . . My sacrifice, O God, is a broken spirit; a broken and contrite heart you, God, will not despise"* (Psalm 51:2, 10, 17).

"God, I am broken and contrite," I prayed. "I am Mephibosheth. Wash me and cleanse me, Lord. Make me new. God, I was wrong. I've made so many mistakes. Take my selfish pride. I give you what's left of my life to use however you see fit. Teach me to love the way you love. I just want to eat at your table and be a reflection of you in all I do."

41

Nick was different. There was no mistaking that. Everyone noticed, especially Abbi. And it was quite sudden. Like Moses coming down from the mountain, there was a glow about him. Gone were the anger and cynicism, replaced by a quiet confidence that Abbi had to admit she found curious and intriguing. Yet she was still cautious, wondering how long it would last before the old Nick reared its ugly head.

Outwardly, circumstances were not getting any better, not by a long shot. In some ways, they'd been getting worse. Abbi wanted to trust God. She knew Romans 8:28—had quoted it her entire life. *"We know that in all things God works for the good of those who love him . . ."* What good? She couldn't see it other than the change in her husband. But a new attitude wouldn't bring Philip back or pay the mounting bills. Abbi could tell

Nick wanted to break through to her, but she was a stone wall. Instead of pushing, however, Nick gave her space.

Abbi stayed out of Nick's office most of the time. After he came home from the hospital, she only had to go in there periodically. Because the house was so huge, Abbi had her own quiet spot in the opposite wing and came in and out via the garage. They'd stopped dropping Nick off out front, so she rarely passed through the foyer or by his office.

This particular night the voice was back, along with the panic and insomnia. *"Abigail, don't be fooled. You know the real Nick. He's let you down too many times. What makes you think he's any different now?"* Abbi punched the pillow next to her, barely missing Deuce. He drew back startled and confused. "I'm so sorry, boy," she said, pulling him up to her chest, nuzzling him. For the last few nights Deuce had been sleeping with her, as if he could sense her struggling. Some nights he slept with Nick. Deuce was a link between them.

Frustrated at the voice in her head and angry about not being able to sleep, Abbi decided to get up and walk again. One thing was certain. She couldn't stay in the bed. This time, she carried Deuce in her arms, caressing him, speaking softly to him. He was a warm and comforting companion.

Walking through the ten-thousand-square-foot house it seemed cold, more like a hotel lobby than a home. *Do we really need all this?* Abbi thought. *It's ridiculous.*

Deuce suddenly growled, then squirmed to get down. He took off limping, his wild barking echoing down the hall.

"Deuce, shh," Abbi said, following him. "You're gonna wake everybody up!" But Deuce continued to run and bark. Abbi finally caught up with him in Nick's office, where he suddenly became calm and sat under Nick's desk.

"Figures," she said. Then she noticed Nick's Bible open on his desk, the torn pages taped back together. Normally Abbi would have been thankful, but now a cold stiffness rose up in her. "Good for you," she mumbled out loud, "but what about the rest of us?" She looked down at Deuce. "If only I were more like you," she said. There was a part of her that wanted to forgive Nick, to make things like they were before. But there was one thing standing in her way. It was like a bottomless canyon ripped across a mountain path. Abbi knew the way, knew where she needed to go, but she couldn't get to the other side. The canyon was too deep, too wide. That canyon was Philip. Abbi could handle the bankruptcy, Nick's recovery, even his long-term disability. She could start over from scratch and forgive him for what he did to Deuce. But not Philip. The bitterness over her son's death ate at her like a cancer.

"Love the whore!" she yelled up at the ceiling. "Love the whore!" Now she didn't care who she woke up. What he did with Philip's situation, to Philip, to her—that was betrayal. "I know what you told me to do, God, but I can't!" She took her hand and knocked the Bible back on the floor. Deuce ran out of the room. "I've tried and I can't do this!"

I know you can't, my daughter. Just as before, the still, small voice inside her was unmistakably clear. She knew it was God speaking to her heart. *Only I can through you. You need me, Abbi. You need to depend on me as your source for everything.*

Abbi dropped her head into her hands, her throat constricted. "God, help me." Her voice cracked.

Deuce's tail started wagging under the chair, thumping her foot. Abbi looked up to find Nick standing in the doorway, leaning on his walker.

"How long have you been standing there?" she asked, wiping her eyes with the back of her hand.

"Just a few seconds," said Nick.

Abbi willed herself to focus on his eyes, on his face. "God better hurry up, Nick," she said, then turned away to look out the window where the sky was just beginning to lighten.

"Abbi?" Nick said softly.

Ignoring him, she continued to stare into the front yard.

"I release you." Nick couldn't believe the words that were coming out of his mouth. His heart wanted to hold on. He wanted to take her in his arms and press his lips to hers. "I understand if you need to leave. I really wish you the best. I want your happiness."

A full minute passed without either of them saying a word.

"Why did you have to change?" Abbi finally spoke, her voice barely a whisper. "Why couldn't you have stayed a jerk? It would have been easier."

42

It was a big deal. Maria had insisted.

Abbi and I tried to talk her out of it, but she would not take no for an answer. As a farewell gift, Maria prepared us a feast. We both figured she had more up her sleeve than food, and we were right! It was supposed to be the four of us: Maria, Carlee, Abbi, and me. But at the last minute, Carlee had a mysterious errand to run, leaving me and my wife sitting at the candlelit table. It was a total setup! Of course, Deuce was sitting under the table waiting for any scraps that might get dropped accidently on purpose. Standing between us, Maria took each of our hands and escorted us to our seats.

The table was set in the formal dining room off the kitchen. Lights were dim, candles lit. Soft music played in the background. She had gone to great lengths to create just the right atmosphere. Of course, she declared that this was a formal dinner and we would have to dress accordingly. I wore dress jeans, a black silk shirt, and a black sports jacket. It was the first time I'd dressed up since the accident. And Abbi, *wow!* She wore *the* red dress. It was my favorite and she knew it, which confused me. Why would she wear that dress when she knew it made me crazy for her? The red dress was the perfect backdrop for Abbi's auburn hair, emerald eyes, moist lips, fair skin, and the pearl necklace. She wore that too! One thing was for sure, I needed to do whatever I could to make things right! *What a fool I've been,* I thought. *She needs to know I'm crazy about her.*

"Maria, you shouldn't have done all this," said Abbi.

"It's an honor to serve you," said Maria. She wore a festive Spanish dress, makeup, and jewelry, her hair pulled back into a bun.

"Maria, you look charming," I told her.

"Thank you, Señor G," she replied. "Now sit."

Abbi's best china was set on the table with crystal water glasses and polished silverware, a fresh bouquet of flowers in the center.

"Hold hands," Maria ordered. She held out her hands and we all connected, making a circle. I thought Maria was going to pray, but she squeezed my hand for me to take the lead. A lump rose up in my throat. Sometimes it was easier to pray in front of twenty thousand strangers than two people who know everything about you—the good, the bad, and the ugly.

"God," I stammered, "cover us with your mercy and grace.

We need you. Thank you for Abbi and all she's endured because of me. Thank you for Maria. We are so grateful for her help and we love her. Amen."

When I looked up Abbi's eyes were moist. Maria's too.

"I'll be back," said Maria, leaving Abbi and me in awkward silence. It was difficult to keep eye contact with her. Not a minute after Maria left the room, the music switched to the Rod Stewart classic song, "Have I Told You Lately." Like the red dress, it was *our* song. How did Maria get this information? Carlee! Midway through the song I held out my hand across the table for Abbi to take. She didn't take it, which left me hanging. "You're still the most beautiful woman I've ever laid my eyes on, Abbi," I said, undeterred.

She looked up, into my eyes. "Thank you."

"Abbi, you know you're the one," I said, my voice already beginning to tremble. "You always have been and always will be."

Her eyes darted away, down to her plate.

"I've made so many mistakes," I said. "My priorities were upside down. My loyalties were misplaced. I thought my decisions were protecting certain people, but they were tearing others apart. I hate what I did and who I was. I don't want to go back to the old me."

Abbi looked like she wanted to believe me but wasn't completely convinced.

"I want Nick Gregory to die—and I don't mean suicide," I said. "I want to die to myself and let Christ live through me.

That's where we were when we started out. I don't care if I push a broom the rest of my life. I just want to love the people God brings in my life. Abbi, I'm telling you, the old Nick is dead."

Abbi reached out her hand and took mine. My heart skipped a beat. I thought my pacemaker might go into defib. "Oh Nick," she said, "I wish I could believe you, but I'm sorry. I don't. Right now I don't know what I feel."

Everything in me screamed to defend myself, to force her to talk to me. "It's okay, Abbi," I said instead. "It's really okay. I understand." In my heart I knew it was going to take a miracle resurrection of Abbi's heart for her to love me again.

"I'm going to check on Maria," Abbi said as she wiped her mouth and set her napkin down.

43

The meal was one of our favorites. It was Maria's top-secret family recipe. Abbi and I pushed through the event for Maria's sake. This time I was pretty certain Abbi was wearing her photo smile. Being a pastor's wife had given her plenty of practice with that. She'd learned to smile and say "Praise the Lord" when her heart was being stomped on. God, I loved that woman! I suspected Maria could see right through it, but she chose to go along with the charade . . . until the end, that is.

"Señora Abbi, Señor G," she said, hands on both hips. "I've worked for you over ten years. That's a long time. You think this is easy on me?" Maria pounded her chest with one fist, her emotions rising. "I'm going to say what I have to say because you can't fire me now!"

"We would never fire you, Maria," said Abbi. "You're family."

"I agree," I said.

"Good, then," said Maria. "The enemy has been playing both of you. You should know better. His schemes are sneaky." She turned her laser focus on me. "Señor G, I'm going to start with you. Do you realize what Señora Abbi has gone through for you? She's fought by your side for years! You need to love this woman like Jesus loves you. Fight for her! Stop feeling sorry for yourself. Enough with the self-pity! It keeps the focus on you."

Class was in session. I nodded in humble silence, my mouth stopped.

Maria shifted her attention to Abbi. "Now, Señora Abbi, you know how much I love you. And I'm not telling you what to do, but God has spoken very clearly to you, twice. You told me yourself. Stop trusting your emotions and trust God." Maria paused, looking at the two of us, her eyes flames of concern. "All right, I am finished now," she said.

"Come here, Maria," I said, standing up. She and I embraced. Abbi followed and we had a three-way hug. Deuce jumped in between us completing the circle.

Abbi stepped back. "Thank you, Maria," she said. "I'll consider your words."

Reaching into the antique buffet, I pulled out a gift-wrapped box. "We have a little something for you," I said, handing it to her.

Maria took the gift and shook it. *"Qué es esto?"* (What is this?)

"It's just a little gift to show how much we appreciate you."

"You've done so much for us," said Abbi, "and whatever happens we are going to totally hang out. So this is not good-bye."

Inside the box, Maria found a bright red and yellow multi-colored sarong. She held it up with a puzzled look on her face. *"Oh es hermosos,"* (It's beautiful,) she said. Then she saw the envelope with her name on it.

"There's more," said Abbi. "Go ahead, open it."

Maria opened the envelope and pulled out a brochure to a Hawaiian resort, along with two round-trip airline tickets. "No. No," she said, shaking her head. "It's too much!"

"Trust us," I explained. "I had a lot of points to get rid of or lose. And we have connections for the resort."

"You are sure?"

"Very sure," said Abbi.

We all hugged again. Maria wiped her eyes with her apron. I slipped Deuce a piece of steak under the table.

44

"Okay," said Ray, "push!" I was flat on my back, knees bent. Ray had his hands on my legs, leaning his body weight down on my shins, squeezing them back to my torso.

"Argh!" I groaned, pushing with all the resistance my muscles could give. Ray held my legs until they trembled, then released them. "Whew." I exhaled as my legs relaxed.

Ray stood up. "That was good, Nick," he said. "You're definitely getting stronger, and your coordination is coming along as well."

I sat up on the floor and took a long gulp of my Dasani, then held out my hand for Ray to grab and pull me up.

"Nope," he said, looking down, arms folded across his chest. "I want you to struggle. You know the saying, 'Where there is no struggle, there is no growth.'"

"Frederick Douglass," I said.

"Hey, I read, too, you know," said Ray. "Speaking of struggle, it's time we take it up a notch."

"Great . . . I can't wait."

"No more walker." He grinned.

"What?"

"That's right. From now on, strictly crutches."

"Next thing you know you're gonna have me loading my own furniture in the U-Haul."

"I'm sorry about all that, Nick," Ray said, empathy lingering in his voice. "It must really stink. You know, losing everything."

"It's tough," I said. "But losing stuff is nothing. It's losing people—that's the toughest." I took in a long gulp of water, emptying the plastic bottle and crushing it in my hand. "Never take the people in your life for granted, Ray. You hear me?"

"Yes sir," said Ray. "I hear you."

"Okay, enough preaching," I said. "The preacher in me still wants to come out every now and then. I guess it's habit."

"You'll be back. I'm counting on it."

"Don't hold your breath," I said. Attempting to change the subject, I placed my arm around his shoulder and asked, "When can I drive?"

"Soon as you get these crutches conquered," he said, handing them to me. They'd been leaning in the corner for over a month. "Then we'll see about driving."

"I hate these things," I said. "They hurt my shoulders and arms."

"Learn to love them, Nick," said Ray. "Besides, they will help build up your upper body. You'll have arms and a chest like the Incredible Hulk."

"I prefer Iron Man," I said.

"Hey, my offer still stands, if you need help moving your stuff."

I waggled my eyebrows. "You just want Carlee to see your muscles."

"I'm counting on it."

"You know she's not allowed to date until she's thirty," I joked, "and then only in a group—a church group."

"Those church girls can get wild," he said. A big smile came across his face. "You know I'm—"

My cell phone started ringing. I checked the name, *Kenny Squires.* "Excuse me, Ray, I need to get this."

Ray stepped out.

45

"Hey, Kenny," I answered.

"Nick, my brother!" said Kenny. "How are you?"

"Better than I deserve," I said.

"Good answer," said Kenny. "Do I hear traces of the Nick I know and love?"

"A lot's happened since we last talked," I said. "Why are you so hyper today?"

"I'm excited about what God is doing . . . and . . ." He paused to create suspense.

"And what?" I braced myself.

"Have you and Abbi found a place to move into yet?"

"We found an apartment near Baltimore, less expensive than Great Falls, but nice. Anything's going to be a step down." I chuckled. "More like an escalator of steps down."

"I see."

"We haven't moved yet. We're supposed to sign the lease agreement this week."

"Before you sign—"

I cut him off. "Kenny, I need to tell you something before you go any further." I paused to gather myself. "Abbi may not move with me. She's seriously considering moving to her parents' in Texas."

"Wow. Looks like I called at the right time then," he said. "I'm just going to lay it all out. I think this may be a God thing."

"Whatcha got?" I said, sitting down on the workout bench. "I could use a God thing about now."

"You know that piece of land I own outside of Tulsa?"

"Yeah, you bought it to build your dream home on."

"One day," he said. "But not for a while. It's about 150 acres. Really beautiful. Got a spring-fed creek running through it. Some woods. Nice pasture."

"I've seen the pictures, Kenny. It's beautiful."

"Well, there's a house on the property. It's not much, more like a cabin. Got a nice wraparound porch and it's under a cluster of oaks. Quaint. She's screaming for a little TLC, though. Linda and I have been staying there some on the weekends. We've done a little work on it. But . . ."

Please hurry up and get to the point, I thought. Sometimes Kenny liked to go around the block to get next door.

"I was thinking about renting it out," he continued, "but . . ."

I was silent.

"I want you and Abbi to have it."

"What do you mean, 'have it?'"

"I'm not exactly sure what the long-term would be, but for now, I'd like you to live in it rent-free for as long as you need to. I'm talking years if that's what it takes. There's plenty of room on the property for us to build when we're ready."

"Kenny . . . I . . ."

"Wait, there's more!"

"More?"

"All right, are you ready for this? You may want to sit down."

"I'm sitting."

"I have another offer for you."

A lump rose up in my throat. "Another offer? The house is over the top, Kenny."

"Well, this is even bigger. You ready?"

"You're killing me here, Kenny! I'm ready."

"I want you to be the associate pastor at my church."

"I . . . uh . . . I don't know what to say," I stammered. "You do know who I am, right? Nobody wants to touch me with a ten-foot pole right now."

"I know exactly who you are, Nick, and I don't kid about things like this. The church is a far cry from Grace Life. We're only running about three hundred, but we're growing. God's doing a special work here. I'm having a hard time keeping up and could really use your help. Whatcha think?"

"It's . . . humbling," I said.

"I know. Isn't it great?" He laughed. "Going from twenty-thousand members plus television audience to associate pastor at a small church nobody's heard of has got to be humbling."

"I wasn't thinking of it that way," I said. "Actually, I meant I'm humbled that you asked me—that you would trust me to be your associate pastor. The offer sounds wonderful. It's just . . ."

"Just what?"

"Do you think they'll have me?"

"Nick, come on, the name of our church is The Healing Place—'where no perfect people are allowed.' It's full of broken people who need a healing touch from God. Of course they'll have you!"

"Well, I qualify then. I'm a broken mess."

"That's why I want you," said Kenny. "To be used mightily, a man must be broken deeply. I don't fully trust anyone who hasn't had their faith tried through tough times."

"Thank you, Kenny," I said. "We'll pray about it. It might be just what we need."

"That's all I can ask for," said Kenny. "But listen to the Holy Spirit. This is a real opportunity. And, Nick?"

"Yes."

"Deuce is gonna love it!"

46

Abbi looked through the bedroom window and saw the sun was just beginning to peek over the trees, the house still. Nick was asleep in his room and Carlee in hers. She'd come home for the weekend and Deuce chose to sleep in Carlee's bed that night. Abbi looked at the clock. She knew it was too early, but she was desperate. Abbi had to have answers because she was about to make one of the biggest decisions of her life. She picked up her cell, scrolled through her contact list, and pressed Call. After four or five rings, someone answered.

"Hi, Abbi," the man said, clearing his throat. "It's been a while. Are you okay? It's so early."

"I need to talk to you," said Abbi.

"Okay, let's talk."

"In person."

"Sure. What day do you want to come in?"

"Now."

"Now? Don't you think this is a little impulsive?"

"Yeah, it's impulsive," she said. "But I'm desperate! And I'm not coming to your office either. I don't want the attention. Meet me at Starbucks on Georgetown Pike in an hour . . . Please."

"I don't know, Abbi. I've got a full schedule."

"After all we've been through! You be there."

"All right," he said reluctantly. "One hour."

"Thank you."

Abbi wore jeans and a sweatshirt, no makeup, and her hair pulled back with a headband. She snuck out while everyone was sleeping. Nick couldn't follow her anyway—he wasn't cleared to drive. She pulled up the hood of her sweatshirt and adjusted her big, round sunglasses. Since they'd sold the Lexus, she took the van. Abbi didn't think the media would catch on, but so what if they did?

Abbi seated herself so she had a clear view of the door and waited, sipping her latte.

He walked into the Starbucks looking rough with a scowl on his face and hair sticking up like he'd skipped the shower. Of course, his wife was in tow—he had to do everything by the book.

"Hi, Cindy. How are you?" said Abbi, a polite gesture.

"Abbi, are you okay?" Cindy said, hugging her. "What's going on?"

Abbi smiled her photo smile at Cindy, then glared at Al Champion. "Look, I don't have time to play games."

"What has brought you here today, Abbi?" Al said. "How can I assist you?"

"Don't talk to me like we're in a counseling session, Al. Let's just cut through the small talk," said Abbi. "Give me one good reason I should stay with Nick after all he's put our family through. You've spent more time with him than anyone."

"I know he adores you, Abbi. You are his—"

"Trophy wife?" Abbi snapped.

"No, certainly not," said Al, "more like his warrior wife."

"If I'm all that, why didn't Nick tell me about Philip? He was my son. I could have helped him."

"Good question, Abbi. But here's an even better one. Why didn't Philip tell you? Why did he tell his dad and not you?"

Abbi felt like she'd been slapped. She had secretly asked herself that many times. "Because he's *the* Nick Gregory!" she blurted out.

"How about this? Philip loved you and didn't want to break your heart, or maybe he was too ashamed?" Al said gently. "Why didn't you realize something was amiss? You were his mother. Maybe some of this anger you feel is anger at yourself for not picking up on the clues and not being the one Philip felt he could talk to. Maybe you need to accept a little responsibility yourself, Abbi."

"How dare you lecture me about responsibility! I didn't do anything wrong. I was a good mother. I've always been the one faithfully standing by, doing all the right things."

"Abbi, you know better than to sit here and pretend it was all Nick's fault. There is none righteous—not one. As long as you're parading your anger and righteous indignation around, there's no room for God to speak into your life and illuminate those areas that he wants to heal."

"Don't preach to me, Al! This is about Nick. How could he let this happen? He should have been outraged. He should have done something!"

"We all have blind spots, Abbi. You, me, Nick. It's easy to see in retrospect what should have been done. Nick was devastated when Philip told him what happened. He was ready to go kill the guy. But Philip was so ashamed and depressed, he didn't want the attention this thing would draw from the press. Abbi, if you were abused would you want the whole world to know?"

Abbi was silent, tears of anger pressuring her eyes.

"Philip had been living with it for several years before he told his dad," Al continued. "Nick felt like he had to do what was best for the ministry so that more people were not hurt over this tragedy. Obviously, it wasn't the right decision, that's clear now. His judgment was clouded by the concern he felt for those he thought would be hurt more by making it public. He's guilty of looking after the thousands rather than the one—Philip. That doesn't make it right, but it doesn't make him a monster either."

"I should have been told, Al. I was his mother." Abbi turned her burning eyes at Cindy. "You're a mother. How would that make you feel? Tell me, Cindy."

Cindy's head dropped. "Not good."

"That's right," said Abbi. "All Nick cared about was himself and his ministry! What about other potential victims?"

"The man was fired and repentant," said Al. "He submitted to serious counseling."

"Why are you taking Nick's side?" Abbi demanded. "I mean, he didn't exactly treat you like a loyal friend."

"I'm not taking sides," said Al. "God is allowing Nick to be broken. My word to you would be to let God finish his work in him."

"His being broken is breaking all of us!"

"Maybe God's doing a work in all of us," Al said, taking a sip of his coffee and then setting the cup down. "Look, I can't tell you whether you should stay with Nick or whether you should leave. That's between you and God. But you and I have counseled enough people to know that reconciliation only works when both parties are broken before God and are seeking him first. When two people who love the Lord are willing to love each other as Christ loved the church and gave his life for it—then they can experience a supernatural healing in the relationship. But it takes two. Are you willing to accept the grace God has to offer for your broken marriage? Are you seeking God first?"

"Oh, now it's about me? Just how did this get to be about me?" Abbi slid her sunglasses back on, stood, and turned to walk out. "Look, I shouldn't have come here. It was a mistake. Good-bye."

"Nick's not the only one God's working on here, Abbi," said Al.

47

Home was the last place Abbi wanted to go. She thought Al would at least empathize with her, give her a little consolation, and validate her feelings. But no, he'd turned things around on her. She was furious—that seemed to be her constant status these days.

Driving in this state of mind was probably not wise, but she was feeling a little reckless. "God, why is this happening to me? What did I do to deserve this?"

She realized the road she was on and would soon be driving past the spot where Nick had rammed the Escalade. "What an idiot," she murmured, angry with him all over again. She thought if he'd just finished the job, she wouldn't be in this predicament. It was an awful thing to think, but she was flying unchecked, indulging every ounce of anger she could muster.

"You could end all your pain, Abigail. You could see Philip. Just do it. End the pain. Be at peace. You know you want to be with your son. They took him away from you."

Philip. Philip. My son. Abbi tightened her grip on the steering wheel, focusing her anger on the accelerator, on Nick, and pressed down—70 mph, 80 mph, 90 mph. Flying over the highway, she was free at last.

"It would be so easy, Abbi, just turn the wheel slightly and it would all be over."

"No! In Jesus' name! Leave me!" Abbi screamed to the voice.

A sliver of reason materializing, Abbi eased off the accelerator. "What are you doing?" she said out loud to herself. "Get a grip."

Taking the next exit, Abbi continued three miles on the boulevard, turned left, and drove along the curvy, tree-lined road that led to the only place she could think to go. After turning in the driveway, the car tires crunched on the gravel as she navigated through the maze until she reached her destination. Parking the car, Abbi walked the rest of the way to Philip's grave. She chided herself for not bringing fresh flowers when she saw the ones she'd left last month had withered. Without the slightest hesitation, Abbi dropped to her knees on Philip's grave and wept.

"Why didn't you tell me?" she whispered, her voice tired and hoarse. "I could have helped, sweetheart. I could have helped you. Why didn't you tell me?" Emotionally and physically exhausted, Abbi rested her arms and head on the tombstone while staying on her knees. Though still a bit chilly, the warm spring sun felt soothing. Closing her eyes, she dozed off until a hand touched her on the shoulder.

"Mom."

Abbi's eyes squinted open and she looked up. "Carlee? What are you doing here?"

Sweatpants, sweatshirt, and hair tousled, Carlee was standing there holding Deuce. "When I woke up, something inside told me to go to Philip's grave. I just needed to come."

She set Deuce down and he limped to Philip's gravestone, made an awkward circle, and plopped down beside it.

"I miss him so much, Mom," Carlee said, bending down, caressing the picture of her brother embedded in the granite. He was dressed in a tux—it was his senior picture. Underneath the picture was his epitaph.

Philip Carson Gregory
Son, brother, friend
Deeply loved, greatly missed.
"It broke our hearts to lose you
but you did not go alone
for part of us went with you
the day God called you home."

"I miss him, too, honey," said Abbi, standing up and touching Carlee's shoulder.

Carlee turned and fell into her mother's arms. Abbi held her daughter tightly as they wept together. A few moments later, Carlee pulled away, nose red and stuffy. "Mom," she said, "I think you should go to Tulsa."

"What?" Abbi replied, a bit caught off guard. "What brought that on?"

"I've wanted to tell you," Carlee said. "Seeing you both like this is killing me—first Philip, then Dad's stuff, now this?" She wiped her eyes with the sleeve of her sweatshirt. "I know you still love him. I can see it."

"This is not about love," said Abbi.

"Really, Mom," said Carlee. "That is so lame and I don't buy it for one second."

Abbi looked at her daughter. "It's complicated," she said.

"Yeah, right. It's only complicated because you're making it complicated."

"Your dad betrayed me and you, Carlee. I'm not sure I know how to get over that. There's been too much water under the bridge."

"You know, if I got a word directly from God I think it would help me get over that bridge," said Carlee.

"You've been talking to Maria," said Abbi.

"Thank God for Maria. She's helped me through this."

"What about me? You can talk to me."

"Mom, I'm talking to you now and you're not hearing me,"

said Carlee. "The bitterness and anger is killing you. I hardly recognize you anymore. You're not the same mom."

Unable to respond, Abbi stared at her daughter and shook her head.

"So everything you taught me growing up about God's love conquering all, and his forgiving our sins as far as the east is from the west, is just a bunch of baloney? What about all those stories about how you and Dad met, that God brought you together and that he called both of you into the ministry? God must've made a big mistake! Is that what you are saying? That God's a liar?"

"Carlee!"

"You say you believe, but the way you're behaving doesn't show it."

"Carlee, what about you? How can you just let your dad off the hook for what he did?"

Carlee grew quiet, then lowered her gaze. "Mom," she said, "there's something you need to know. It's about Dad."

"Okaaay," Abbi said slowly. *What could Carlee possibly know that I don't?*

"I don't think he's the reason Philip did what he did."

Abbi appeared confused. "What do you mean?"

"He told me what happened," said Carlee.

"Who told you what happened, your father?"

"No. Philip did."

"Philip?"

"Yes ma'am."

Abbi began to shake. Clutching her stomach, she felt like she'd been pricked with a thousand needles. "Philip told you that he had been abused?"

"He told me everything, Mom."

"And you didn't tell me?" At first the words came out choked and stifled, then forceful and loud. "How could you keep something like that from me, Carlee? Don't you think I deserved to know what went on with my own son? I can't believe you." Her face flushed and hot, the volcano inside erupting, Abbi slapped Carlee across the face. "You, your dad, Al— you all betrayed me!"

Carlee stared wide-eyed at her mom in disbelief, her cheek red and burning. Sensing the tension, Deuce jumped up and limped between them.

Abbi looked down at her hand like it was a foreign member. Wetness forming in the corners of her eyes, she couldn't believe what she'd just done. "Carlee, honey, I'm sorry. Please, I didn't mean it. Forgive me, baby." Abbi reached for Carlee, but she jerked away.

"Philip made me swear not to tell you," she said, "because he knew what it would do to you." At that, Carlee took off of running to her car.

"But I could have saved my son," Abbi whispered as she watched her daughter drive away.

48

While she was standing there dazed, Abbi's cell phone dinged, indicating a text message. She looked at the name. *Karen Young?* she thought. *Last time I saw her was at Nick's party.* Abbi read the text. *"Hey, Abbi. Here's a video I thought you may want to see. I took it at Nick's party."*

Abbi sat down on a nearby bench and downloaded the video. It was the day Nick came home from the hospital. He looked so frail and a little out of sorts. He was clearly not expecting a room full of people when he got home. Then the "Yelp!" Abbi knew what was coming next, but watching it on video made her heart tighten.

Precious Deuce walked in with his doggie cart, looking a little out of sorts himself. He stood there waiting for Nick—everyone in the room stood frozen waiting to see what would happen next. When Nick whistled and Deuce took off for him, it pricked Abbi's heart. The love and devotion Deuce showed Nick—it was all there caught on video. There was a subtle shift inside Abbi.

Abbi closed out the video and slid the phone in her jacket pocket. She looked at Deuce, who was sitting in his cumbersome way by Philip's tombstone. *How can he forgive and act like nothing happened?* she thought. Then she remembered her conversation with Dr. Conroy when she first visited the clinic after he'd been hit. The vet had said many pet owners would have chosen to put down animals injured as severely as Deuce.

"Never!" Abbi had said. "Deuce is here for a reason. I know it. He's needed." *Maybe teaching me to let go of this anger is one of his reasons?*

Abbi started walking back to the van. Deuce stretched out his broken body and hobbled behind her. "Deuce, what's it going to be?" she said. "Are we going to Tulsa with Nick?" Deuce looked up at Abbi, his tail wagging.

49

We couldn't kick that dog off the front porch. Kenny was right about one thing: Deuce loved country life. So did Abbi. The house was an old wood-frame structure with only two bedrooms. It was maybe one thousand square feet. Kenny and Linda had knocked out some walls to make a great room with an open kitchen. An island with a countertop and stools separated the two areas. There was a stone wood-burning fireplace and lots of windows, each with a picturesque view of the 150 acres of trees and pasture.

The outside of the house was painted forest green to blend with the environment. Topping it off was a tin roof and a huge wraparound porch. Did I say huge? The porch had more square feet than the house itself! Sitting on the porch, it seemed our closest neighbors were about a hundred Black Angus. True to

Kenny's words the house needed some TLC, but Abbi's nesting instinct kicked in and she rolled up her sleeves at the challenge. As a welcome gift, in addition to helping us move in, some men from the church showed up to do carpentry work and painting. The women helped Abbi turn the house into a home.

When all the work was done and our furniture in place, it was quaint and warm. Most of all, it was peaceful. There was a quiet presence about the place that was therapeutic. In the evening you could sit on the front porch and see stars stretching forever while listening to the coyotes in the distance. Kenny assured us the coyotes wouldn't bother Deuce if we kept him inside at night. True, the garage at our mansion back in Great Falls was bigger than our whole house now, but there was something here that was different. It was honest, humble, and grace filled. A few years ago I would not have considered living in a place like this. It would have been beneath me. But something was happening to me. In addition to my new understanding of grace, each day I was being freed from the need of excess stuff. It's amazing how much stuff we had that we didn't even need. The simple life was freeing. It had been nine months since the crash and I was actually healing faster than the doctor had anticipated. Though I walked with a severe limp and needed the aid of a cane, and sometimes the walker, I could even drive now for limited stretches and purchased an old pickup truck that came in handy around the farm.

A country girl at heart, Abbi, like Deuce, felt at home from the moment we set foot on the property. Parting with stuff came surprisingly easy for her. The hardest part for Abbi was leaving Philip's grave and, of course, Carlee.

My solace came from limping around the property slowly with my cane, praying and taking notes, Deuce usually limping by my side. We'd walk to the spring-fed creek, where Deuce loved to wade and catch floating leaves. That dog loved the water. Occasionally, I still used the walker when my muscles grew weary. The walking was my exercise. I did my own physical therapy now, going in to Tulsa once a week for intensive therapy.

Abbi found solace in her garden. God spoke to her while she was out there. "There's something spiritual about the feeling of soil in your hands," she said, wiping them on her faded jeans. "Planting seeds in the ground, tending and nourishing them, and then watching them grow out of the earth like babies is a miracle." The more time she spent in the garden, the more peaceful Abbi became. The garden also gave her space from me. I mean, it's kind of hard to hide in one thousand square feet.

Our relationship was far from healed, but Abbi was trying to make it work. The difference was she now had faith that in time it could be healed. When she made the decision to come to Tulsa, it was more than a choice to move; it was a choice to trust God, to dive in headfirst. We still slept in separate bedrooms and hadn't kissed, nor had she told me that she loved me.

My job was clear, to win my wife back not by words, but by actions. And unlike in D.C., Abbi was giving me a chance. My goals had been boiled down to this: I must decrease and Christ must increase in every area of my life. I just wanted to love people and for them to see Christ in me, starting with my wife.

50

"You know what amazes me about Deuce?" I asked Kenny. He was sitting in the swing on the front porch. I was in a big white rocking chair eating sunflower seeds, spitting the hulls into an Oklahoma Sooners mug. Abbi and Lisa had gone inside to check on dinner. Kenny nodded at my question.

"He runs all over this property but never goes too far and always comes hobbling right back to where he is now."

"You better be careful that you don't rock over his tail." Kenny chuckled.

"Exactly," I said. "There's no fences to keep him in other than the barbed wire for your cows, but he can go right under those. Deuce is absolutely free to run away, but he doesn't. He always comes back."

Kenny adjusted his hat and switched his toothpick from

one side of his mouth to the other. "Here's a story for you," he said. "You can put it in one of your books."

"I told you," I said, spitting a load of seeds into the cup. "I'm through writing."

"That's funny." He laughed, slapping his thigh.

"I'm serious," I shot back. "Nobody'd publish me anyway. They wouldn't risk getting their books pulled."

Kenny slid off the swing and got down on one knee. "Come here, boy," he called and then whistled. Deuce just rolled over on his back, legs in the air. "Oh, I see how it is. You're getting spoiled, aren't you?" Kenny scooted beside Deuce and scratched his belly. "How many lessons has this dog taught you, Nick?" asked Kenny, looking up.

"I could write a book about them," I replied before even thinking about it.

"Bingo!"

"Stop it. That was just a figure of speech."

"*Law* and *grace*," he said, patting Deuce, then standing up. He leaned against one of the knobby cedar porch columns. "Pretty simple when you think about it. If you put up a chain-link fence in the backyard and made Deuce live in there, all he'd be doing twenty-four-seven would be obsessing about that fence and how to get out. Every time you opened the gate, he'd be more interested in escaping than spending time with you. That's what living under religious rules and law is like. They make you fence conscious. Yet, with no fence and all this space, Deuce is free to roam. He's not fence conscious. He could run off anytime he wants and never come back, but he doesn't. He keeps coming home. Why? Because he's not thinking about running off, he's thinking about his masters. He loves you guys. Instead of being fence conscious, Deuce is Nick and Abbi conscious. It's his relationship with you that keeps him on this porch. Think about that."

"Good word," I said.

Abbi stuck her head out the screen door. "Dinner is ready."

I held the door open for Kenny, then for Deuce.

51

"Come look at my babies," Abbi giggled, grabbing my hand and pulling me.

"Slow down," I told her. "I can't walk as fast as you, remember?"

"Hurry up, old man!" she shouted, looking back.

I picked up my pace, taking a step, swinging one leg out and forward, then taking another. It was awkward and humbling, but I managed.

Pumpkins.

Abbi loved her pumpkins. It was early August now. When she wasn't filling her bird feeders, she was tending her pumpkins. Of course, she had planted other things—like squash and cushaw. But she loved her pumpkins the most. And Abbi went all-out. She didn't have a couple of pumpkin plants. Abbi had a pumpkin patch, a big one! Four rows, twenty-five yards each. Why pumpkins? I had no idea, other than Abbi loved them. Not to eat, but to look at, decorate with, and give away in the fall.

I had to admit, I was seeing a side of Abbi that I'd never seen before in the whole twenty-five years of our marriage. How could I have missed this? As the plants blossomed, so did she. And I liked it. In the past, I'd thought she was beautiful, but watching her in the garden, wearing ragged jeans, my button-up shirt several sizes too big, straw hat, dirt caked on her face and hands, standing with a hose watering—well, that was just plain sexy. Abbi was changing too. She didn't talk much about it, but she hadn't withdrawn into her shell. She was more peaceful and relaxed. The simple, slower life was freeing us both.

"Look at this one!" she said, pulling back a pumpkin leaf, revealing a dark green/light green baby pumpkin about the size of a tennis ball. "It's going to be as big as a bowling ball this fall!" Abbi clapped her hands with excitement. Deuce was barking at a squirrel in the background. He had found a new calling in life, too—to keep the Gregory family protected from squirrels. And Deuce took his job seriously. He couldn't run very fast with his limp and I felt certain the squirrels knew it and exploited the situation.

"It's green," I said. "I've never seen a green pumpkin before." My lip formed a thin smile.

"It'll turn orange when it's ripe, silly. Come on! Let's count them!" Abbi grabbed my hand again and guided me through the patch, lifting leaves searching for baby pumpkins. When we had spotted the fourth or fifth one, it suddenly occurred to me that Abbi was touching me. She was holding my hand and continued to do so through the entire tour. This was major!

"That's thirty-one, not counting the duds," said Abbi, letting go of my hand.

I wanted to hold it forever, pull her to myself and engulf her, shower her with kisses and tell her how much I love her. "That's a lot of pumpkins," I said instead. "What are we going to do with them?"

Abbi got a mischievous twinkle in her eye. "Well," she said. "I was thinking that when they're ripe this fall, you and I can bring the church kids out. They can pick some and we can paint and carve designs on them! And we could have a bonfire and a hayride and roast weenies and marshmallows. We'll probably have at least fifty or sixty pumpkins by then!"

"Abbi," I said softly, "you're pretty amazing. You know that?"

"Shh," she said. "Look over there in the grass. It's a bunny."

I could tell Deuce wanted to chase it, but he showed great restraint and remained still. We had trained him not to chase the rabbits, but let him have his way with the squirrels.

52

My phone sounded like a pinball machine indicating text messages and missed calls. I was in the habit of powering it off at night and turning it back on first thing in the morning. I was letting it come to life while showering. I could hear the *ding, ding, ding, ding* from under the water flow.

"What in the world?" I said, turning off the water and grabbing the towel. *Ding, ding, ding.* I looked at the phone—11 missed calls! 19 voice mails! 22 text messages! It wasn't even 8:30 a.m. yet. My first thought went to Abbi. Was she okay? She was out for an early hair appointment that morning. I scrolled through the list of missed calls: Al Champion, Frank Redfield, *Frank Redfield?* Maria, Kenny, Carlee, and a host of others. Just as I was about to pull up one of the text messages to read, a new call came through. It was Kenny.

"Kenny," I answered. "What is going on? Is everything okay?"

"Turn on the news and you'll find out!" he said. "Fox News. God's at work, Nick!" He laughed and hung up. *That was strange.*

Wrapped in my bath towel, I limp-hopped without my cane the twentysomething feet from the bedroom to the living room, clicked on the television, and turned it to Fox News.

"About Nick Gregory," the *Morning Show* anchor said. She turned to her colleagues sitting next to her. "That was such a great story," she said.

"Yeah," replied one of the other anchors. "That was a nice break from the intense election coverage."

"When we come back, we'll have this season's winner of *The Voice* right here in the studio, so don't go away."

"What?" I yelled. "What *about* me?"

Flipping through the channels and stopping on ABC, NBC, CBS, and CNN, all of them had nothing on but commercials or election coverage.

Ding, ding, ding—my phone was still going off in the bedroom. After hobbling back, I picked up the phone and pressed Call.

"Hey, Daddy!" Carlee said. "This is sooooo awesome! Only God!"

"What's so awesome?" I asked. "What's going on?"

"You don't know?"

"No, I woke up, turned my phone on, and I've got tons of messages!"

"Dad, your video went viral! All the major news channels picked it up. People are going crazy over it!"

"Not again," I moaned, falling back on the bed. "That was almost a year ago. You'd think they'd just let it go!"

"Dad," said Carlee, "I don't think you understand. It's your new video."

"What new video?"

"You know, the one of you and Deuce at the party when you came home from the hospital?"

"Carlee, I don't know what you're talking about," I said. "There was a video of that?"

"Yes. Mom didn't show you?"

"No."

"Someone at the party took it on their cell phone and sent it to Mom."

"Well, I haven't seen it."

"It's amazing, Dad! Go to YouTube and watch it. The news is calling it the 'Feel Good Story of the Year'!"

"Wow, you mean the public doesn't hate me?" I asked with a tone of sarcasm.

"Hate you? They love you!"

"All right then," I said. "I'd better go watch it."

"Hey, Dad."

"Yeah."

"I have some other good news."

I perked up. "You got your fiancé back?"

"Ugh, no, Dad. I wouldn't take Marshall back if he begged me." Carlee paused. "I'm coming to Tulsa for a visit, and . . ." She paused. "There are a couple of master's programs out there I'm looking into."

"Now, that is really good news!" I said. "The best news."

As soon as I hung up, I went to YouTube and typed in *Nick Gregory dog video*. My two dog videos came up along with page after page of old Nick Gregory preaching videos and Nick Gregory hate videos. They were all mixed together. I watched the first one again, the sixty-seven-second rant that started all of this. Not my finest moment. As I watched, my heart squirmed as I felt the full weight of my foolishness and the pain I'd caused to everyone—to Abbi, to Carlee, to myself, not to mention to Deuce. Even after this long it still hurt to watch it. Who was that guy? I thought for a moment about how far I'd come from then to now. To those on the outside looking in, I was a complete failure. Once a big-time author and mega-church pastor, now I lived in a tiny cabin in the country, served in a small church, walked with a limp, and lived the simple life. To be a failure, why did I feel so rich? Abbi and I were not reconciled, though we were making strides. I still missed my son terribly. Some days the pain of his absence just about took me down. Yet, when I looked in the mirror I actually started to believe in the man I now saw, the one God was crafting. Daily, I could feel God's hand molding this lump of clay. He had to smash it first, but he was making me new, full of grace and confidence in him. I was learning what Maria had said to me daily, to desperately depend on God. It actually was a relief to turn things over to God daily.

Pulling up the second video, its title was the single word "Forgiveness." My eyes watered up as I watched. Tearing up had become my new normal. I often felt like a wimp about it, crying at the least little thing. Abbi would respond, "No, Nick, your heart is becoming tender."

The video sent me back to that day months before. Like I had been, Deuce still looked a mess. Most of his coat had been shaven, and he looked extremely thin. He had several bandaged wounds. His two back legs were fastened to a doggie cart, allowing him to move.

"Yelp." Deuce still stood in the door opening to the great room, waiting, unsure.

"Here, boy!" I called. Deuce stood frozen and then looked at Abbi as if asking her permission. She said, "Go, boy!" But he still didn't move. My heart sank.

"Deuce, come, boy!" I called again, this time patting my thigh and whistling. At that, he took off running as fast as his front legs could directly toward me, pulling his cart. When he reached my wheelchair, he put his paws on my legs and tried to jump up in my lap but couldn't make it. A friend picked him up and placed him in my lap.

"I missed you so much, boy!" I said. I remembered wanting to squeeze him and pat him hard and scratch him vigorously like I knew he loved, but because of his soreness I had only caressed him gently. Crawling up my chest, Deuce excitedly licked my arms and face, then laid his head on my shoulder. "Deuce, my buddy," I cried. "My little buddy. You came to me! I'm so sorry. Please forgive me." Lost in the moment, there was nothing but Deuce and me, my friend, my companion, and forgiveness, lots of forgiveness.

All of it caught on video.

Why hadn't Abbi shown me? Who uploaded it? I wondered, *somebody from the party? Several people there were taking pictures. Maria would probably know.*

I got dressed and walked onto the front porch. Deuce was lying in the sun. I picked up his red ball and tossed it into the grassy field. He just looked at me lazily. I sat down on the steps and scratched his head before heading on to the church. I would take time to read all the texts and listen to the voice mails later. They probably all said the same things anyway. I was preaching on Sunday and had a sermon to prepare for.

53

When I turned into the parking lot at The Healing Place it was jammed with reporters and news vans. I shook my head. *How fast does news travel these days? We're talking not even forty-eight hours.* I took a deep breath preparing for the onslaught of questions but had nothing to fear any longer. My reputation was in God's hands.

Stepping out of the Ford 150, the old door creaked and I had to slam it extra hard to shut.

"Tell us about Deuce," a reporter asked. "What do you think of the new video?"

"Did he really forgive you?"

"Deuce is an amazing little fella," I said, walking toward the church doors. "We would all do better if we could be more like Deuce."

"When can we see you and the dog together?"

I laughed. "I don't know about that."

A reporter yelled, "Stories are flooding in from across the nation, people saying they're changed after watching the video!"

I stopped in my tracks. "What?" I said, whipping my head around. "What do you mean?"

"Stories . . . they're flooding in from everywhere! Facebook and Twitter are going wild!"

"What kind of stories?"

Several reporters started scrolling on their cell phones.

"Here's one from Twitter!" a reporter shouted. "'I felt #hope and decided to give life another shot. #DogForgives.'"

A lump formed in my throat, my eyes doing the familiar watering thing.

"Listen to this one from Facebook," another reporter yelled out. "'I couldn't forgive my husband. I was so angry with him for what he'd done. But when I saw Deuce forgive Nick Gregory, I knew I could forgive. Anonymous.' There are dozens of stories here. Can you comment?"

I shook my head. "All I can say is I'm unworthy and I'm grateful for God and Deuce's grace. You know, when everything came down I made some bad choices. I felt like a dead dog, crippled and worthless. But King Jesus . . . he invited me to his table anyway."

The reporters looked confused by my comments.

"I have to go now and prepare my sermon," I said walking with my limp inside the doors of the church building.

Kenny was waiting in the church lobby, grinning.

"I bet you didn't figure on this circus when you hired me," I said.

"What are you talking about, Nick? It's great publicity for the church and the gospel!"

"What do you think about all of it?" I asked.

"I think God is resurrecting some dead things," he said.

My eyes narrowed. "Did you upload that video, Kenny?"

"Nope. Not me. Didn't see it till this morning."

"I forgot you weren't even at my party."

"Look, Nick, why don't you take the day off? You have a lot to deal with right now."

"I have a sermon to prepare," I said.

Kenny gave me that *Duh* look. "You've preached thousands of sermons, Nick. You can just pull one off the top of your head."

"All the same, right now I need my office."

"Okay, my brother, just remember to keep in step with the Spirit. Like I said, God's up to something."

"Do the reporters know where I live?"

"I haven't told anyone," said Kenny. "The place is hard to find if you don't know where you're going."

Sitting in my office trying to study, I kept looking at my cell phone, the curiosity getting the best of me. I had turned it off after viewing the videos because I didn't want to be distracted and knew it would take me a while just to go through all the messages. I turned on the phone and waited for it to come up. *Ding, ding, ding, ding, ding* and on it went, more messages and voice mails. The last missed calls were from Frank. So instead of listening to his voice mails, I called him.

"Hey, Frank. This is Nick. What's up?" I said as if I didn't already have an idea.

"Nick, my friend! Publishers will be lining up wanting a crack at the new Nick Gregory! You're the feel-good story of the year. I can sell you now! We've got a chance to get it all back, my man!" He didn't even catch a breath. "We have to ride this wave! You're hot again. This video is going to continue to grow. What do you say?"

"Okay, Frank, I'm only going to say this one time, so you better listen up. I'm finished writing! I'm content right where I am. Besides, once this blows over, they won't have anything to do with me. We're over. Good-bye."

Click.

I decided to give up on trying to study and started filtering through my messages. No way could I listen to or read all of them. Noticing my brother Charles had left a voice mail, his was the first one I listened to.

"What's up, country boy?" said Charles, his voice gruff from years of smoking. "You got any deer on that property? How 'bout getting us a buck for Thanksgiving? Topeka's only four hours away. Now you have no excuse." He turned his mouth away from the receiver to cough. "I saw your video, big bro. Looks like God's giving you a real message."

"Thanks," I whispered to myself. Al Champion was next.

Since he'd left a couple of voice mails and several of the board members had as well, I figured I needed to at least listen to his.

"Hello, Nick, hope you are doing well," Al said. "I saw your video. Great stuff. Looks like it's going viral. The church is buzzing over it. Congratulations, buddy. Oh, one more thing. It looks like there's not going to be an investigation regarding Philip after all. Attention is on the elections and now that you're everyone's hero again, no one wants to hear about it. Whew. Bless you, brother. Let's catch up sometime."

All over one video? I thought. Of course I knew how these things worked. I knew the damage one video could do. Al's words made me want to hurl. It amazed me how easily public opinion could be swayed at the drop of a hat and how differently people treated you when the bottom falls out. I wanted no part of it. I thought again about the last part of Charles's voice mail: *"Looks like God's giving you a real message."*

It seemed to me it was more Deuce's message than mine.

54

Stopping at the metal cattle gate, I pushed the remote and let it slowly swing open. When we'd first arrived in the spring, we had to get out and manually open it. Since then, because it was such an ordeal for me to get in and out, we bought an inexpensive electric opener. Waiting for the gate to open, I couldn't help but compare this gate to the one back in Great Falls. This one was metal connected to a barbed-wire fence and wood posts. The one in my former life, just the gate and wrought-iron fence alone around my property cost more than Kenny had paid for this entire 150 acres, including the house!

It was not even noon yet. After a couple of hours of trying to focus on my sermon, I decided to take Kenny's advice and go home. Things had gotten pretty wild at the church. The phone had been ringing off the hook with the press and others inquiring if I was really the assistant pastor.

I don't know if it was because of my physical limp and my broken life, but the press treated me differently than before. Instead of being hostile, they were gracious. Maybe they were surprised to see Nick Gregory crippled and driving an old pickup truck. Maybe they felt sorry for me. I didn't care. I was past the point of being insulted.

Easing down the gravel road weaving through the pasture to the house, I drove past cows grazing and saw Abbi and Deuce in the pumpkin patch. She looked up from the fifty or so bright orange bowling balls and waved for me to come. I turned the truck and drove through the bumpy field to the patch. Deuce's tail started wagging a mile a minute and he hobbled to the truck waiting for me to crawl out.

"Hey, buddy," I said, patting and scratching him until he seemed satisfied.

"You're home early," said Abbi.

"It's been an unusual morning," I said.

"Really?" she said, sounding sincere. "Tell me about it."

How did Abbi not know anything? Impossible. Surely reporters had called her too. Then it occurred to me that she'd been gone all morning. "You don't know what's going on?" I asked.

"Come here!" she said excitedly, ignoring my question. "You've got to see this one!" Abbi grabbed my hand and pulled me through the pumpkins to this one gigantic yellow and orange one. It was probably the size of three bowling balls! "What do you think?"

"It's a winner," I said. "Blue ribbon for sure."

Abbi bent over and broke off the stem. "Here, help me carry it to the truck. I'm putting this bad boy on the front porch."

With my cane in one hand, I managed to contort my body to where I could lift up on the pumpkin with my other hand alongside Abbi. I wasn't really helping. She was doing most of the lifting. I think she wanted me to feel like I was helping.

"This thing must weigh fifty pounds," I said as we shuffled sideways, facing each other. "No way could I carry this thing by myself."

"Me either," said Abbi. "That's why we're a team."

With our arms still full, I managed to open the tailgate and we ever-so-carefully set the pumpkin down. Abbi wiped her hands on her jeans and then turned to look me straight in the eyes. Her emerald jewel-like eyes were sparkling, sweat drops on her nose and a smudge of dirt on her cheek. "I need to tell you something, Nick. And you need to hear me out."

"Sure," I said.

"It's time you got back to doing what you've been called to do . . . and I'm talking about writing."

"You!" I said. "You're the one who posted the video!"

Abbi lifted a finger to her cheek and smiled softly, most definitely *not* the photo smile. "You got a problem with that?" She leaned over and kissed me on the cheek.

I staggered at Abbi's words, at the idea that she was the one behind the new video and her kiss. Oh yes, the kiss! *Did Abbi actually just kiss me?* My knees got weak and palms sweaty, heart pounding as if I'd just run a hundred-yard dash. But it was great! The pacemaker was definitely doing its job! I studied my wife for a moment. Then I blurted out, "I have to go. I need to be alone with God for a while. There's still plenty of daylight left. Deuce and I are going to the creek and I'm not coming back until I've settled some things." Opening the truck door, I pulled out the wooden stepladder I'd made for him, and patted the seat. "Come on, Deuce. Get in, boy."

55

Tahlequah Creek was a rock-bottom spring-fed water supply lined with pebble and sand beaches that ran for miles on both sides. It served as a natural border to the western side of Kenny's property. Directly across the creek from Kenny's land was over a thousand acres of forest owned by the Boy Scouts, which protected it from development.

Deuce and I drove the pickup as far as we could through the pastures, but then we had to park and walk the rest of the way. Both of us limped through the woods to the beach. I found the perfect spot and unfolded my canvas chair and just sat for a while holding my taped-up Bible, journal, and pen, listening to the songs of nature—the wind blowing through the pines mixed with the sound of birds chirping and rapids running over rocks in the creek. I took a deep breath and listened and waited. Being out here was therapeutic.

After a time, I opened my Bible, turned to 2 Samuel 9, and read about Mephibosheth again. I was particularly drawn to verses 11 and 13: *"So Mephibosheth ate at David's table like one of the king's sons. . . . And Mephibosheth lived in Jerusalem, because he always ate at the king's table; he was lame in both feet."*

Setting the Bible in my lap, I pondered those words. "Lord," I said out loud, gazing up at the clouds floating above the treetops, "I want to eat at your table. I thank you for all the grace and mercy you are showing to me, but I don't know about this writing thing. I'm a broken mess, a crippled failure." Picking the Bible back up, I continued to read, this time verse 12: *"Mephibosheth had a young son named Mika . . ."*

I thought about that for a little while. Right between verses 11 and 13 the writer throws in that Mephibosheth had a young son named Mika. What did that even mean? For one thing, it meant that being crippled didn't stop Mephibosheth from accepting David's offer, moving forward with his life, and having a family. In fact, the Hebrew meaning for Mika is "Who is like God?" Mephibosheth named his son "Who is like God?" Though he still walked with a limp, God restored to Mephibosheth everything he'd lost and gave him a brand-new future.

Thinking back to my study of this Bible story in seminary, I remembered that in other kingdoms of the world, Mephibosheth would have been an enemy of the state and

killed, but in David's kingdom—and in God's kingdom—
things are done differently. Though Mephibosheth was broken
and felt worthless, King David still wanted to show him love
in honor of the love he had for his father, Jonathan. That's why
Mephibosheth got to eat in the palace every day just like one
of the king's own sons. God loves us like that. He can take the
most broken of men and give them a future. That's why he
named his son Mika. Mika represented the new thing God was
doing in Mephibosheth's life.

With my old, tattered Bible in hand, I got up and paced
along the sandy creek bank in deep thought. Deuce was explor-
ing, digging furiously in the sand, but never straying too far.
I remembered that King David himself, who was a man after
God's own heart and who was used as a tool of grace in God's
hand, was crippled in his own way and in need of the same
grace from God. David committed adultery with Bathsheba.
Then, on top of that, David had her husband—one of his faithful warriors—set up in battle to be killed. Later, David's sin was
exposed and there were grievous consequences. Bathsheba and
David's son became deathly ill and he begged and pleaded with
God to let his son live. David spun into deep depression and
grief, refusing to eat.

Boy, could I relate. The weeks and months following
Philip's death I was insane with grief. In spite of David's pleading with God, his son died. I flipped in my Bible to 2 Samuel
12 and began reading in verse 20:

"Then [after grieving for seven days] David got up from the

ground. After he had washed, put on lotions and changed his clothes, he went into the house of the LORD and worshiped. Then he went to his own house, and at his request they served him food, and he ate.

"His attendants asked him, 'Why are you acting this way?...'"

"He answered, '... Why should I go on fasting? Can I bring him back again? I will go to him, but he will not return to me.'"

I could not bring Philip back, but one day I would go to him in heaven. "Philip was a believer," Kenny told me. "He loved God. You should know that more than anyone, Nick. He was struggling. You know that. I think the enemy just deceived him into believing suicide was the only way out. You can understand that, right? We know suicide is never the answer. Our days are numbered by the Lord and we should never take our lives into our own hands. We short-circuit the Lord's timetable for our life. We each have a purpose to fulfill. Each of us is a unique creation before God, and he uses the things we go through to prepare us for what he's called us to do."

David's sin was great, but God's grace was outrageous. David married Bathsheba and they had another son—Solomon. God worked through a union that began in sin to birth the great King Solomon. Chew on that for a while.

God had gifted me with the ability to speak and to write. I had been in a position of influence and used that to cover up Philip's sexual abuse by one of our youth pastors. The decision was made to quietly dismiss him because we didn't want to cause more pain to Philip, the members—but really it came down to the negative publicity. I went along with this rather than doing the right thing, calling the authorities, making Philip's healing and recovery my highest priority. And I should not have hidden it from Abbi. Keeping that secret from her violated everything our relationship stood for. I was more concerned over my own career and ministry than Philip's pain. Keeping it from Abbi was just to ensure it wouldn't blow up because I knew she would *not* be silent.

What Philip needed to know was God's love and mercy and forgiveness. He felt shamed and needed my embrace. He only needed me to understand his struggle, to not be ashamed of him, and to love him more than my ministry and the church. You have to understand, the ministry was huge, all consuming. I let it consume me and didn't have time for my own son. Less than a month later, Philip overdosed. The guilt I felt over the next year was beyond torture. I kept it together by pushing forward with work and ministry. People were getting saved. The church was growing. My books were selling. Each day it was becoming easier to push my dark secret to the back of my mind. Then Abbi found the note Philip left and everything started to unravel—her moving out and filing for divorce, my rant in the front yard, running over Deuce, losing the pastorate, and then finally driving the Escalade into the pylon.

Right there on the creek bank, I felt myself being sucked back into the black hole of depression and self-hatred.

"If it weren't for you, Philip would still be here," the voice said. *"You deserve to suffer. And what makes you think God will*

use you for anything again, Nikky? He's finished with you. You've wasted your life believing this brainless garbage. And what makes you think people will read your stuff anyway? They know who you really are. They still hate you. They're not going to forget everything just because of one little video. Plus, you're a cripple. Give it up, Nick. You're a loser and always will be."

"Shut up in Jesus' name!" I yelled, my voice echoing across the creek. "I live by the power of God in me now!" Deuce stopped his digging and looked up at me. I picked up a rock and angrily skipped it over the water, then picked up another one. The second it left my fingers a different voice, gentle and peaceful, spoke from deep inside my spirit.

Let me birth a Solomon in you, Nick.

Instantly I knew what it meant.

"But, God," I stammered. "I can't. I'm worse than Mephibosheth, worse than a dead dog." A gentle breeze brushed my face. I felt God was downloading a special message into my spirit. I picked up my journal and began to pen the following words.

My son, let me use your sin and past mistakes. Refusing to receive my forgiveness is a sin too. Now that you are broken, you are ready. I called you to write—that hasn't changed. Everything you've written to this point was merely preparation for your deepest work. This is not the end, but the beginning. Pick up your instruments of labor and regain your confidence in me. Go back to your secret closet of prayer. Trust me to provide for you. Writing is no longer your dream, but your assignment. Obey me. Finish strong with a limp, a victorious limp.

I breathed in the nature around me. Standing on the side of Tahlequah Creek I was overwhelmed with peace and calm flooding my soul, washing me with wave upon wave of grace, shattering the darkness, sending the depression into oblivion. The long season of silence was over. I confessed to God and he was pouring life into my spirit.

Then the words *Dead Dog Like Me* formed in my mind. This time, however, they didn't come to me as a name belittling me. I knew the words were to be the title of my next book. Yes, I am Mephibosheth.

56

A lot had happened in the month since the second video went viral. Frank was right. Publishers were lined up and salivating for *Dead Dog Like Me*. Several had already offered significant advances, but Abbi and I were taking our time on this one. We had prayed for God to show us the right publisher and the right literary agent to work with. God's answer came in the form of an older gentleman who had spent a lifetime in publishing and had huge success, but now only took on projects he felt had eternal impacts. He was more interested in the message than the messenger. That's what we wanted as well. Frank seemed really upset when we decided not to go with him.

Abbi and I stayed at The Healing Place to worship, but I stepped down as associate pastor to devote myself full time to writing and speaking. Of course, I made myself available to

Kenny and the church. Our plan was to use the book advance money to buy the house and a portion of Kenny's land. He, in turn, could purchase the adjacent hundred acres he'd been eyeing for a while. This was home now, especially since Carlee was moving to Tulsa, which was pretty amazing. When I moved back into the bedroom with Abbi, the second bedroom became my office with a fold-out sofa bed for Carlee when she came to visit.

* * *

"That sure is a nice crop you got there," I said to Abbi. We were sitting on the front porch sipping our coffee, looking out over her pumpkin patch. It was a crisp fall Oklahoma morning, the sun beaming down. The green growth in the field had died back, leaving dozens of bright orange balls dotting the ground.

"Yep," she said from the swing. "Good crop."

"We need to get the kids out here to pick them and have that bonfire," I said from one of the rockers.

"I would like that," said Abbi. Two blue jays chased each other around the porch, one landing on the bird feeder.

"I'll talk to Kenny and set it up."

"Nick?" Abbi said softly.

"Yeah?"

"I love you."

Savoring the moment, I closed my eyes and rocked. "I love you, too, Abbi."

Deuce brought his red ball and dropped it at my feet. "It's early, boy," I said. He just looked up, tail wagging with anticipation. I picked up the ball and tossed it into the front yard. Deuce hobbled after it.

Author's Note

There were two Mephibosheths in David's life. One was killed. That Mephibosheth was not Jonathan's son referred to in 2 Samuel 9. Sometimes people confuse the two. Also, there are two theological views about Mephibosheth referring to himself as a "dead dog." One view is that he was showing honor to David. The other is that he had a low view of himself. After extensive research, I believe it was a mixture of both and chose to go with the latter for the sake of the story. Finally, the Bible alludes to a lifetime of tension between Ziba and Mephibosheth. I took creative liberty and imagined possible scenarios.

Acknowledgments

I would like to say a special thank you to . . .

Ted Squires: What can I say? Coach, you know how to get it out of me. Agent, you're in a league of your own. Friend, I'm honored and humbled.

Jeana Ledbetter and Jennifer Stair, for taking this story to the next level and making me a better writer.

Leonard Davidson, you know why.

Worthy Publishing and their team of rock stars, for taking on this project, working so hard, and believing in the power of story.

Alanna, my wielder, thanks to you we're hitting our targets!